THE HOCKEY PLAYER'S HEART

AN M/M HOCKEY ROMANCE

JEFF ADAMS

WILL KNAUSS

BIG GAY

THE HOCKEY PLAYER'S *Heart*

JEFF ADAMS & WILL KNAUSS

London Borough of Hackney	
91300001151503	
Askews & Holts	
AF ROM	£6.49
	6561821

THE HOCKEY PLAYER'S HEART

Hometown hero. Hockey superstar. Perfect boyfriend?

When hockey star Caleb Carter returns to his hometown to recover from an injury, the only thing he's interested in is a little R & R. He never expects to run into his onetime crush at a grade school fundraiser. Seeing Aaron Price hits him hard, like being checked into the boards. The attraction is still there, even after all these years, and Caleb decides to make a play for the schoolteacher. You miss 100 percent of the shots you never take, right?

Aaron has been burned by love before and can't imagine what a celebrity like Caleb could possibly see in a guy like him. Their differences are just too great. But as Aaron spends more time with Caleb, he begins to wonder if he might have what it takes to win the hockey player's heart.

The Hockey Player's Heart
Copyright © 2018 by Jeff Adams & Will Knauss
All rights reserved.

Editor: Kiki Clark, LesCourt Author Services
Cover Design: Meredith Russell, meredithrussell.co.uk
Formatting: Leslie Copeland, LesCourt Author Services

2nd edition, 2020 from Big Gay Media
1st edition, 2018 from Dreamspinner Press

PROLOGUE

IN HIS TWO years on the Foster Grove High hockey team, Caleb Carter had faced off against some of the biggest and baddest players in the state of New York. But nothing he'd ever encountered on the ice could have prepared him for what he was about to do.

Alone in his bedroom, Caleb tried to control the sudden, sickening panic that gripped him. Why was he freaking out so badly?

Because he had zero experience talking to guys the way he wanted to talk to Aaron tonight.

Practicing the positive visualization technique that Coach had taught the team, Caleb inhaled deeply, gulping down what should've been a calming breath. He glanced at the digital clock on his bedside table and knew he'd wasted enough time. It was now or never.

He reached for the doorknob, then paused, brought his hand to his face, and breathed into his palm. Deeming his breath acceptable, he headed downstairs.

Caleb stopped on the stairway landing and peered through the railing at everyone assembled in his family's

1

living room. Balloons and a giant banner hung above the fireplace mantel. Only a few pieces of the graduation cake his mom had made were left.

Earlier that afternoon, Caleb and about a dozen members of his extended family had sat in the bleachers at the high school's football stadium and watched his older sister, Pam, and her best friend, Aaron Price, graduate with honors. The ceremony seemed to go on forever. But when Pam took the stage in the middle of the field and gave her valedictorian speech, even he had to admit it was pretty inspiring.

Afterward, everyone came back to the Carter home for a joint family graduation party. Caleb had hoped to find a moment to talk to Aaron alone, but Aaron and Pam dealt with a seemingly endless array of relatives. Each one had to congratulate them and discuss college plans and their respective futures.

Aaron now stood at the bottom of the stairs, laughing at something his uncle was saying. When the older man eventually turned away, Caleb called down, "Hey, Aaron, do you have a second?"

"Sure," he answered before bounding up the steps to where Caleb stood. "What's up?"

"Can I talk to you?" Caleb asked, gesturing for Aaron to follow him into his room.

At the end of the hallway, music blared from behind Pam's bedroom door. Pam had escaped the party to change out of her dress. She and Aaron would be leaving soon for the Safe and Sober Grad Night party.

Aaron stood expectantly in the middle of Caleb's room, hands in the pockets of his dress pants. He wore a nice button-down shirt and tie, his dark hair combed neatly and parted on the side. Caleb thought he looked great.

"You okay? You've been acting strange all afternoon," Aaron said.

Caleb's mouth went dry. He tried to casually shrug off the question, but all that came out of his mouth was an aborted squeak.

He had to get a grip. This was Aaron. His sister's best friend. He had to be cool.

"So, I, um. I got you something."

"You didn't have to do that."

"Yeah, I did." Caleb went to his desk, opened the drawer, and pulled out a brown paper bag. "Something to say thank you. Sorry I wasn't able to get it wrapped. We only had Christmas paper and that seemed weird."

Aaron took the package Caleb offered and looked inside. A huge smile spread across his face, and it warmed Caleb far more than he'd expected.

Aaron removed a small trophy from the bag. It was a cup, with handles on either side. The wood base had a gold plaque that read: *Aaron Price—World's Best Tutor*. Caleb had bought it at the pro shop located next to the ice rink where he practiced every morning. He even spent the extra money to have it specially engraved.

"I wouldn't have made it through geometry without you, and if I'd flunked, I'd be off the team."

"You're the one who did the work."

"But you spent all those hours helping me, drilling it into this thick skull of mine."

"Caleb, I wish you wouldn't say things like that. You're a lot smarter than you give yourself credit for."

"Anyway, you're the reason I know the difference between equilateral and isosceles triangles. I wanted to give you something to show you how much I appreciate it. You're a seriously good teacher."

Aaron held the little trophy up, admiring it, turning it so it glinted in the late-afternoon light that shone through the bedroom window. "I love it."

Before he could second-guess himself, Caleb stepped toward Aaron and gave him a hug. He'd intended for it to be a quick embrace and clap on the back, but to Caleb's surprise, Aaron wrapped his arms around him and didn't let go.

Time seemed to momentarily stop. He wanted to squeeze Aaron and hold on tight, but fear threatened to overwhelm him. His stomach somersaulted, and he didn't want Aaron to get the wrong idea.

Caleb needed to let go.

But he liked the warm feel of Aaron's body underneath that dress shirt.

What was happening?

A moment later, Aaron began to pull back.

As Caleb stepped away, without thinking, he turned his head a fraction of an inch and brushed his lips across Aaron's cheek.

Caleb immediately jumped back, his face burning hot with embarrassment. "So yeah, thanks... For the tutoring, I mean," he blurted out. "You really helped me a lot."

"You're welcome. I'm glad I could." Aaron smiled, his eyes warm and kind. He absently pushed his glasses back up the bridge of his nose. If he felt any of the awkwardness Caleb did, he didn't let on.

There was a loud knock. Caleb glanced over his shoulder as Pam opened the door and poked her head in. "Come on, Aaron. We need to get going." She disappeared down the hall, leaving his door open.

"Be right there." With the little trophy in hand, Aaron turned to leave but paused briefly in the doorway.

Caleb's heart pounded in his chest as he waited expectantly for Aaron to do something, say anything. The moment stretched out for what felt like an eternity. It had taken every ounce of courage Caleb had to give Aaron that trophy. If he gave the gift back, Caleb knew he would literally die of embarrassment.

"Thank you, Caleb," he finally said. "I'll see you later."

Caleb stood by himself and listened to Aaron's footsteps as he returned downstairs to join Pam and take her to the after-hours Grad Night party.

Caleb unconsciously brought his fingertips to his lips. Had he really just done that? Had his lips actually touched the skin of another guy?

Caleb had kissed Aaron Price.

He'd never been so happy in his life.

ONE

Some things never changed.

Caleb drove his luxury SUV down the familiar streets of Foster Grove on his way to grab breakfast.

"Gotta love small towns."

He'd arrived at his parents' house late last night, just before midnight, after a three-hour drive from New York City, where he'd run out of patience with the sports media shadowing his every move, asking when he'd be back on the ice. The team doctor had already provided them the date he was expected back from his broken foot, but the media seemed to think something magical would make it earlier.

Six weeks ago, all it had taken was a fast slap shot to the inside of his left foot. It'd felt like he hadn't even had a skate on as the puck slammed into him, sending searing pain up his leg.

He still didn't know how he'd kept from falling over. He'd managed to keep his wits about him, maintain control of the puck, and clear it out of his team's defensive zone to send the Rangers on a breakaway. Afterward, he'd made the slowest trip to the bench he'd ever taken because any weight on the foot was excruciating.

Now the cast was off, and it was time to get out of town.

His phone rang, and Caleb clicked the button on the steering wheel to answer. He smiled when he saw the name on the dashboard display.

"Big sis!"

"Little brother!" Pam shouted. "I'm guessing I didn't wake you."

"Nope. I've been awake for a while. And, before you ask, I've already done today's rehab exercises, and my foot's doing fine."

"Good to know."

"I'm headed to Paxson's right now. Care to join me?"

"You've gotta meet me at this new place. I'm already on my way there. FG Café. It's on Fernwood and Main."

"Better than Paxson's? But that's always—"

Pam cut him off. "You have no idea. Meet me."

"Okay." He was dubious. "I'll be there in a few minutes."

"You won't regret it."

She disconnected, and Caleb couldn't help but chuckle. Pam had always been the bouncy—and somewhat bossy— one. When they were kids and went to skating practice on ridiculously early winter mornings, she was a chatterbox when all he wanted was a few more minutes of sleep in the car. At least today he was already awake, though he'd never match her energy.

It was weird to be home, especially at this crucial point in the season.

Pam was getting out of her car as Caleb pulled into the parking lot.

Caleb grabbed his cane and carefully maneuvered

himself out of the car. "Pammy!" he called, waving as she strode toward him, her smile wide.

For the next week, he had to make sure he walked with measured strides, using the cane until he got used to putting his full weight back on his foot. He knew the drill. It wasn't his first broken foot, but it was the worst break he'd had in nearly twenty-five years of playing.

"It good to see you." Pam hugged him, careful not to disturb the cane.

"You too, sis."

"You look well. Rest and rehabilitation must agree with you. Though you could use a haircut," she said, reaching up and ruffling his hair. "A bit shaggy around the edges."

Caleb let out an exaggerated groan. "Not even five seconds and you're already critiquing me. Is this cane up to your high style standards?"

"Oh, stop." Pam gave him a playful swat on the shoulder. "It's good to have you home. Come on. Let's get inside so I'm not late for school."

"This is impressive. Doesn't even look like it belongs here." He took note of the changes on the block. Apparently, at least a small part of his hometown had changed.

A shoe store had anchored the busy street corner when he'd been here last summer. The overall shape of the building was the same. New stonework on the facade gave it a classic but updated look.

"It opened in the fall. The café runs late into the night, with coffee and pastries, which are to die for. The restaurant serves lunch and dinner. This block has transformed, adding galleries and even a small theater," she explained, as if she worked for the Chamber of Commerce instead of the local school district. "Foster Grove attracts tourists now, especially to the restaurant.

People from Albany come here to eat." Pam opened the door for Caleb.

"Thanks," he said, not the least bit embarrassed for the assist. As they stepped inside the café, he was assaulted with the most tantalizing scents—dark roasted coffee, rich aromatic cinnamon, fragrant vanilla. He turned to Pam with wide eyes.

"Yes." She nodded. "When I tell you something is going to be good, you better believe it." At the counter, she ordered their coffees and a cinnamon bun. "You know, you could've stayed at my place." Pam maneuvered them to a table, and Caleb settled in a comfortably upholstered chair.

"I'm fine," he assured her. "I'm perfectly comfortable in my old room at Mom and Dad's. I don't want to be in anybody's way."

Four years ago, when he'd signed a huge contract renewal with the New York Rangers, Caleb had given their parents open-ended tickets for an around-the-world cruise. His mother had always talked of traveling, and his father loved boats. Now that they had retired, Caleb was happy to offer them an opportunity to try new things and see different places. They'd already sailed through several European ports of call and had three more weeks of their voyage left. From the pictures his parents had posted online and the phone calls he and Pam had received, they were having the time of their lives.

Before he and Pam could discuss anything else, their drinks and cinnamon roll arrived. The decadently iced treat was massive.

"That's incredible."

"It's bigger than your head," Pam joked, though it was only a slight exaggeration. They wasted no time pulling off chunks of sticky bun. "So, how long are you in town?"

"A couple of weeks. I'm scheduled to return to the ice for the first playoff game. If things keep going right, I'll be on skates Monday. I'm going to call the rink and see if I can get some practice time."

"I doubt that'll be a problem. You know people will be glad to help. What made you come up here anyway?" she asked, taking a careful sip of her dark roast.

"Even though we've already clinched our playoff spot, everyone's obsessing over whether I'll make it back to the ice in time, wondering if I'll be ready. The sports media has been more like paparazzi lately."

"Well, you are the leading scorer."

Caleb nodded. "It's not like the team has been hurting in my absence."

"They probably miss their captain." Pam made sad eyes at him that nearly made him laugh.

"And their captain misses them." He frowned and tried not to sound too grouchy. These conversations were why Caleb escaped the city. "You know I hate not being able to play."

"I'm glad you're not rushing it like you did after that sprain in eighth grade," Pam said before rolling her eyes at him.

Caleb couldn't help but grin at the memory and Pam's expression. "I can't put one over on the team doc like I could on Mom and Dad. It was stupid, of course, since I ended up out far longer than if I'd just let it heal."

"Well, you're an athlete. Not usually a group known for exhibiting the smartest behavior when it comes to injury."

Caleb raised an eyebrow at her and ripped off another huge portion of the roll.

"So, I was wondering, since you're here, could you do me a huge favor?"

Pam sounded like she was making a request rather than a demand, and he was immediately suspicious. Though they were only eighteen months apart in age, his sister had always had a strongly protective streak when it came to him. Pam, however, wasn't afraid to exercise her position as eldest whenever she needed something.

"What's up?" He decided to play along to see what she'd ask. He was as much intrigued as afraid of what she'd pull him into.

"The school carnival is Friday afternoon, and it would be amazing if you'd sign a few autographs. It's a fundraiser for the after-school sports program. It'd be so perfect if the hometown hockey superstar could be there."

Nervous laughter spilled out before Caleb could stop it. "That's a lot better than anything you made me do when we were in school."

Pam was the principal at Foster Grove Elementary, the same school they'd gone to when they were children. She'd always helped with school events as far back as he could remember. Her involvement usually meant he ended up doing something she needed.

"I promise you'll just be signing stuff, nothing crazy. Unless you want to work the kissing booth too."

"Why would there be a kissing booth at a grade school carnival?"

"I'm kidding, although it would certainly keep some of the parents busy. And if we had a celebrity, someone like you...."

Caleb stared at Pam in disbelief as she seemed to be mentally filing the idea away for future reference. Best to nip that idea in the bud, and quick. "No, thank you. But I'd be happy to do the autographs. Just let me know where to be and when."

"You're a great little brother." She jumped up, came around the table, and hugged him. "Any chance you might donate a few things for the silent auction?"

"Why didn't you ask me to send something up? I mean, I'm happy I'm here to sign in person, but I would've given you auction stuff regardless."

Pam sat back down and shrugged. "You outdid yourself a few years ago with the whole New York trip and game package, so I didn't want to push. But since you're here...."

"Of course." He couldn't help but grin. "I'm sure I can get something good put together."

"Perfect. You're the best! Aaron and I have been pulling our hair out over the last-minute details that have to be dealt with."

"Aaron?"

"Yes. Aaron Price," she said, looking at him as if he'd lost his marbles.

"He's back in town?"

"Oh God, I never told you? His job in California didn't work out. When he told me, I suggested he come back home. He started teaching third grade at the beginning of the school year."

"Well, what do you know."

"He's doing a phenomenal job. I knew he would. The kids adore him, and I'll admit, I love having my best friend back, just like the old days."

Caleb sipped his coffee and tried to picture Aaron Price after all these years. "I hope I have a chance to see him while I'm in town."

"You'll see him on Friday. Like I said, he's been helping with the carnival, helping with the carnival." She checked the time on her phone. "Crap. I've got to go. I'll send you all the details. It's this Friday afternoon," she said pointedly. "See you later."

She got up, gave Caleb a peck on the cheek, and was off like a shot. He wasn't even sure if she heard him say goodbye.

He sat back and took another bite of the delicious pastry.

It felt good to be back in Foster Grove.

He hadn't really intended to do anything other than lay low while he was here, but he was more than happy to help out with Pam's fundraiser. Playing in the youth hockey league and after-school programs had started him on the path to the career he had today. He liked to give back whenever possible.

Caleb pulled out his cell phone and called Grant, his assistant, to arrange to have some items sent up for the event.

TWO

"You've outdone yourself, sis." Caleb looked around the school gymnasium as the final preparations were being made, with students and parent volunteers buzzing around. "I remember the carnivals when we were kids. It was a handful of ragtag booths."

"Now we get each grade to do a booth. We also ask parents to get involved and create the attractions and games. There're prizes for groups that earn the most money. We need the support, so we try to make it fun and exciting for everyone involved."

"I'm impressed."

"Me too," said Grant Paulson, Caleb's assistant, who'd driven up from New York earlier in the day with items for the auction. "I've been with Caleb to professionally created events that aren't half as organized as this."

"We try." Pam beamed with pride.

The gym door behind them opened with a clang.

"Pam, have you seen—"

They turned to find a man who had stopped short in the entryway.

"I'm sorry. Didn't mean to interrupt."

Caleb couldn't believe it. Aaron Price stood before him.

He was more handsome than Caleb remembered.

Gone were the thick black glasses he'd worn in high school. He now sported very stylish frames that suited him nicely. His thick dark hair was swept up off his forehead, and the close-cropped beard was a handsome addition.

"Aaron!" Caleb stepped forward awkwardly, pivoting his weight on the cane, and pulled Aaron into a hug. "Pam told me you were back. It's good to see you."

"I'd heard she'd corralled you into this." Despite his words, Aaron looked surprised. "Thanks for helping out."

"My pleasure." Aaron seemed tense in his embrace, so Caleb clapped him on the back before letting him go. "You know, you guys really can ask for anything, anytime you need it. Grant can have me sign things and ship them here."

"Of course." Grant smiled, looking perfectly happy to have been summoned to Foster Grove with no warning. "It's no trouble."

"Better to have you here, little brother. Let people see the hometown hero in person."

Caleb's cheeks heated. All he did was play the game he loved, and he was lucky enough to make a living at it. There were no heroics involved.

"What all did she have you bring?" Aaron asked.

"I cleaned out the closet," Grant said. "We've got a couple of jerseys, some game pucks, a pair of gloves, a couple different pictures, and even a stick that's seen some gameplay."

"Pam also conned me into wearing one of these during the signing," Caleb said, indicating the game jersey he had on. "She thinks we can auction it off for a higher amount later tonight."

"I'm buying you both breakfast tomorrow. I'll make it worth your while." She smiled and bumped her shoulder against Caleb's.

"She knows exactly how to get me to do what she wants."

A parent came up and whispered in Pam's ear. Pam nodded and quickly gave them their marching orders. "Aaron, can you get Caleb and Grant set up at table twenty-one? Silent auction forms should be there already, and everything needs to be put on display."

"Happy to. Follow me."

Aaron and Grant grabbed the boxes filled with auction items, and Aaron led the way across the gym. Caleb, mindful of his foot, fell in step beside them.

He couldn't help but notice how Aaron's arms flexed against the sleeves of his polo shirt.

"It's good to see you," Aaron said. "Sorry about the circumstances, though."

"It's annoying not being able to play. I should be in Tampa tonight, but injuries happen. I'm happy to be here, though. Otherwise I'd just be trying to avoid the game and making myself crazy."

"Pam says you're here for a couple of weeks."

They stopped in front of a table draped with a colorful handmade banner emblazoned with Caleb's name and set the boxes down. There were auction sheets taped down, plus room to display the various items, as well as space for Caleb to sign autographs.

"The city started to feel like a microscope, so I came here." Caleb studied Aaron now that they were standing still. He seemed nervous, which didn't make any sense.

"Where your sister puts you on display for the whole town."

Caleb shrugged. "Yeah, when she gets an idea in her head, it can be hard to say no."

"Well, if there's anything I can help with while you're here...."

"Tutor me some geometry, maybe?"

Aaron looked momentarily confused, and Caleb couldn't help but chuckle.

"Kidding."

"I wondered for a moment why on earth you'd need geometry to recover." Color rose in Aaron's cheeks.

Caleb turned his attention to the table, hoping to steer them away from his bad joke. "So, what do we need to do so we're ready?"

"Get everything set up on display alongside the forms and keep enough space for you to comfortably sign."

"On it." Grant stepped up to the table and started unloading and arranging items. "How will we know who bought an autograph?"

"People buy tickets, and each ticket has a two-dollar value," Aaron explained. "Pam's priced Caleb's autographed pictures at twenty tickets, and pucks at thirty. If anyone brings something for you to sign or if they want a selfie with you, it's ten tickets. The stick and the jerseys will go during the live auction."

"That much?" Caleb had done high-profile fund-raising events in the past and knew special items brought in high dollar amounts. But that was the big city and usually for a large charity, not Foster Grove Elementary. He wasn't sure the people he grew up with would pay that much.

"I guess so," Aaron said before leaning in to speak quietly. "You're kind of a big deal, you know? Haven't you noticed people stealing glances at you since you walked in, especially the kids?"

Caleb glanced around the room, trying his best to not be obvious about it. There were several kids looking in his direction instead of focusing on their tables, much to the chagrin of a few frazzled adult volunteers.

"People try to play it cool, but if they don't know you personally, it's huge that you're doing this."

"Okay. If someone's willing to donate that much to the school to get me to scrawl my name on something, I'm all for it."

As if on cue, Grant pulled out a stack of glossy eight-by-ten color photos featuring Caleb in his full Rangers gear—blue home jersey with red and white lettering diagonal across the chest. He held a stick across his body as he smiled for the camera. It wasn't his favorite, but as the official team picture, it was what he was supposed to use for this kind of event. He felt he was too primped, with every hair just so and looking perfect for the camera.

Aaron stared at the photo.

"Something wrong with those?" Caleb finally asked.

"They're really good," Aaron said, closely studying the photo. "But hockey players are usually all scruffy and sweaty. This is clearly well before game time."

Aaron preferred his hockey players scruffy and sweaty? Duly noted.

"These are taken at the start of the season, before anything has a chance to get marred—the gear or the player. Nothing ever looks this pristine again. I'd prefer a more real-istic look, especially since this year it's like some doppel-ganger model took my place."

Aaron laughed, and Caleb had to admit he liked the warm sound. "Maybe James Bond is under there. Peel off the gear and there's a tux with a hidden compartment for a martini."

"Now those"—Caleb pointed at the pictures Grant had just placed on the table—"are much better." Grant handed one to Aaron to look at. "This was taken just before a face-off. It's candid, more real. It captures the intensity of the moment."

A young student and parent, with cell phone at the ready, approached them. "Excuse me, Mr. Carter."

"Yes?" Caleb looked down at the boy who'd spoken.

"I'm Heath, and this is my dad. We've been doing some Facebook Live posts to show people what to expect when they get here. Can we talk to you?"

Caleb looked over to Grant and raised his eyebrow. "Do I have an interview scheduled?"

He pulled out his phone and tapped the screen. "Nothing on the calendar, but I think for this young man, we can fit him in."

"I think you're right." Caleb looked to Heath and smiled warmly.

Grant stepped out from behind the table. "Take it easy on him with the questions, okay?"

He nodded vigorously.

"I'm going to leave you with the media," Aaron said. "I've still got some setup to do."

"We'll catch up later," Caleb said before Aaron headed off for a group of students at the third-grade table. He turned his full attention to Heath. "So, what do you want to know?"

Caleb spoke with Heath for several minutes while his dad recorded. When Heath went to find his next subject, his dad stayed behind and told Caleb that Heath was a fourth grader who wanted to be a reporter when he grew up, and that he had taken it upon himself to interview people about the evening.

Once Heath called his dad away for another interview, Caleb and Grant worked on arranging the table so people could easily navigate around it for photo ops.

When had Aaron become so cute and adorable? He hadn't been like that in high school. Geeky-cute, sure, with his thick glasses and wiry-thin look. The intervening years had been good to him. He was lean but muscular. Maybe he worked out, because he certainly wasn't a beanpole anymore. The new glasses and beard really made Caleb take notice.

It'd been more than a year since Caleb had dated anyone, and more than five since he'd been in a serious relationship. He struggled to maintain something since he traveled nearly half of the season, which could stretch to more than eight months if the team went to the playoffs. Even if something serious were to start in the off-season, all too soon he'd have to seriously focus on his game.

Would it be different to date someone who lived in his hometown? He didn't get here often, but it'd be a reason to make sure he returned more regularly. His family would love that, and so would he, really. He loved playing for New York, but the longer he'd been there, the more he wondered if the big city was really for him.

Caleb shoved those thoughts aside when some other parents came up to thank him for helping the school. He'd have plenty of time to consider the possibilities later.

THREE

Aaron returned to his students to help them finish their booth setup.

Even though Pam had mentioned that Caleb would be making a special appearance at their small-town event, it hadn't prepared him to see Caleb for the first time in years, standing in the gym. It was good talking to him again after so long. What had surprised him was the visceral reaction he had to being close to Pam's kid brother like that.

One thing was for certain. Caleb Carter was no longer a kid.

What the hell was happening? Just standing close to Caleb had left Aaron unsettled. Examining those pictures, Aaron had felt the heat coming off Caleb, not to mention the occasional bumps he had gotten as Caleb reached around to point at the images.

The candid picture captured the real Caleb—and it was sexy as hell too. Caleb's sweaty face, a lock of blond hair peeking out from the helmet, showed the effort and intensity of the game. The subtle five o'clock shadow got Aaron's full attention and drew him in. He wanted to see the photo come to life.

Thankfully, Heath, intrepid fourth-grade reporter, had come up and broken the moment before Aaron's body could noticeably react—no blushing, no sweaty palms, and thank God, no tent in his jeans. That would've been the worst.

Caleb looked amazing. Aaron had a pretty good idea about the physique underneath that oversized team jersey he was wearing. Caleb packed solid muscle from all the training he did. It'd been true in high school—he'd seen Caleb shirtless a couple times by accident—and it still had to be that way since he was a pro athlete.

He couldn't think about that. After what had happened during his time in California, he'd had enough of jocks to last him a lifetime.

"Wow. It is true!" An unmistakably loud voice from the next table caught Aaron's attention. Hunter James was the tallest boy in Aaron's class. His height and take-charge attitude made him the de facto alpha male among his group of friends—or at least, Aaron supposed, as alpha as a third grader could be.

Hunter pointed across the gym at Caleb. Josie and Terry, teammates of Hunter's on one of the city's youth hockey teams, looked where he indicated.

Aaron suppressed a chuckle. The kids—in particular these three who were teammates—had been in a state of disbelief since Pam announced two days ago that Caleb would be here. It didn't matter that he'd been seen around town; many students were still sure he'd find something better to do on a Friday night than turn up at the carnival.

"It's true. It really is him," Aaron said.

"And that's his stick?" Terry asked as Grant passed by, carrying a hockey stick.

"Of course it is. What's wrong with you?" Hunter shoved Terry's shoulder. "Why else would it be here?"

"That's so cool," Terry whispered, staring at the stick.

"Hey, Grant?" Aaron called, motioning him to come over. "Would you mind giving these guys a closer look at that?"

"Sure." Grant doubled back and held the stick out to the trio.

"Can I hold it, just for a second?" Hunter asked.

"I don't see why not." Grant handed over the stick, which was taller than either Hunter or his friends. The reverence with which Hunter treated it surprised Aaron.

"Cool," Hunter whispered, as the other two also touched it. Hunter returned it more quickly than Aaron expected. "How much is it?"

"I don't know," Grant said. "It's being auctioned off."

"What's that mean?" Terry asked.

"It'll go to whoever offers to pay the most for it," Aaron said.

"Oh man, I got no chance at that," Hunter said, sounding defeated.

His disappointment tugged at Aaron. "Come on. I can introduce you to Caleb."

"You call him Caleb?" Josie sounded surprised.

"Sure. I've known him for years—even helped him pass geometry."

"No way." Hunter bounced in place, his excitement evident.

"If I knew Caleb Carter, I'd make sure everyone knew it," Terry added.

Grant chuckled, and Aaron couldn't help but smile. He didn't want to dampen the students' enthusiasm, and it was cute how they reacted to the star in their midst.

25

"Are you sure, Mr. Price?" Josie asked, seeming unsure that such a thing was even a possibility. "Can we really meet him now, before everyone gets here?"

"Of course."

As Grant and Aaron began to lead the three of them to Caleb's table, Terry suddenly stopped short.

"Wait up a second," he said, darting back to where he and his friends were working. Terry dug around in his Rangers backpack before pulling out an oversized action figure, Caleb's number emblazoned on the little blue-and-white jersey. Terry quickly rejoined his friends, keeping up a constant but quiet discussion as they approached Caleb, their hometown hero.

Grant quickly went back to work, organizing the auction items as Aaron introduced Caleb's admirers. "I've got three fans here. This is Hunter, Terry, and Josie."

Caleb came around the table, smiling broadly as he saw the group approach. As each of them held out their fist, he bumped his fist with them. "Great to meet you all."

"I'm a center, just like you," Hunter said proudly. The ease he displayed in talking to Caleb led the other two to join the conversation, which quickly led to a chattering cacophony as the three talked over one another in their eagerness to tell Caleb all about their playing.

Aaron enjoyed watching Caleb interact with the kids. He seemed to take a genuine interest even as he was bombarded with information. He'd make a good teacher or coach, and that warmed Aaron's heart.

"Would you like me to sign that?" Caleb asked, pointing to the figure Terry clutched reverently. Terry seemed suddenly hesitant.

Aaron could imagine Terry wasn't particularly crazy

about an adult, no matter how famous, scribbling all over his favorite toy.

He watched as Caleb carefully gauged Terry's reaction.

"How about this?" Caleb asked as he took three pucks off the table. Grant handed him a silver Sharpie. "Now, don't tell Principal Carter that I gave you these, or she'll be mad at me. Keep playing, and hopefully, I'll see you on the ice at The Garden one day." Caleb handed Hunter a signed puck.

"You sure will. Thank you." They traded a fist bump.

"Wow," Josie said as she got hers. "Thanks." Another fist bump was exchanged.

"Awesome." Terry fist-bumped Caleb again when he received his puck.

"You all should get back to our booth and help your classmates get ready," Aaron said, bringing the moment to an end. "We open in about ten minutes."

"Thanks, Mr. Price, for letting us meet him."

"You're welcome."

The three darted across the gym in a state of overexcitement. Grant plucked three more pucks from a bag to rebuild the pyramid he'd made.

"You were great with them. Although, you're right that Pam's not going to like giving away the merchandise."

Caleb smiled. "It's okay. I'll cover for those three."

"Is it strange seeing your face on merchandise, like that toy of Terry's?"

"It's strange at first, but you get used to it, I guess."

As one of the few out-and-proud players in the NHL, Aaron knew how significant it was that Caleb was so beloved by his fans and sought after by companies for merchandising and sponsorship deals.

"I've never known anyone who's had a doll made in

their likeness."

"That's not a doll," Caleb emphasized. "That was a one-sixth scale, collector's edition, premium action figure. The league did a series of them last year."

Caleb certainly wasn't a preening, macho sports star, but Aaron found his insistence on the precise masculine terminology for an NHL doll amusing. He couldn't resist giving his old friend a hard time.

"It sure looked like a doll to me," Aaron teased. "In fact, if we went back to your parent's house right now and dug around in Pam's old bedroom closet, we'd find a box full of Barbies who'd just love to go on a dream date with that miniature version of you."

"Well, as long as Malibu Ken came along, I'd be okay with that."

Aaron couldn't help himself—he laughed out loud.

Caleb chuckled as well.

"In all seriousness," Aaron continued, "thank you for taking the time to talk to those kids. I know it meant a lot to them."

Caleb waved it off as if it were no big deal. "When I was their age, I met Gideon Roark after a game. His team and coach were trying to hurry him along to get on the bus, but he stopped, signed a puck, and talked to me for a few minutes. Dad was with me, and even he said we needed to let him go, but Roark continued to talk and even offered some face-off tips. I still have the puck, and because of him, I always take time for kids. Sort of a 'pay it forward.'"

That was a side of Caleb that Aaron had never seen in the press. "That's a great story. Ever thought of working with kids?"

"I have. Realistically, I'm only viable in the NHL for a few more seasons. Not many play into their forties, and while I'm still a few years away from that, I do think about the future. Maybe I'll coach. I've got good role models. There's my sister... and you."

Aaron was glad he didn't blush easily—fluster, yes, blush, no—because his insides certainly fluttered at that compliment.

Caleb wasn't flirting. Was he? He couldn't be. Caleb had always been nice and that's all the compliment was.

"I, um, should go check on my table." Aaron checked his watch. "I've got parents and kids trying to organize a bake sale that also involves whack-a-mole. They're going to think I've abandoned them."

"We can't have that." Caleb smiled broadly. "Catch up after? I'd like to know more about what you've been up to all these years."

"Um. Sure." That was the last question Aaron had expected.

At the third-grade table, Aaron saw that everything was well organized. He only half paid attention to Susan and Heather, the parents who were helping out, as they told him how they'd arranged everything. Playing whack-a-mole and winning tickets to buy baked treats was fine by him.

Why was he fixated on Caleb? He'd been around him for less than an hour, and he felt like he was back in high school and struggling to hide a crush. Caleb might get along great with kids and want to help them, but he was famous and must have his sights set higher than what went on in a small-town elementary school—even one where his sister worked.

After a rough time, things were finally going Aaron's way. His new calm, quiet life suited him. Caleb would be here for a short time, and then he'd be gone, and everything would be back to normal.

FOUR

Two and a half hours passed quickly, and as far as Aaron could see, the carnival had been a resounding success.

From the moment they'd opened the gymnasium doors, every fundraising table and game station had a boisterous line of enthusiastic community supporters. Everyone involved, kids and parents alike, seemed to have enjoyed themselves.

As the last of the people finally departed, Aaron was pleased to see their bake sale table and all its tasty offerings were fairly decimated.

Pam rallied the proverbial troops—a few teachers and some parent volunteers—and the cleanup crew got to work.

Caleb had proven to be a big draw and had a long line at his table from the time the doors opened. Grant helped a lot —collecting tickets, keeping the line moving, and even making sure Caleb got a couple of breaks. Despite the line, Caleb talked with everyone, took pictures, and signed a ton of stuff.

As Caleb and Grant approached his table, Aaron

noticed that Caleb had ditched his cane at some point during the event and was walking without it.

"So, what's left to do?" Caleb asked. "I'm happy to help."

There really wasn't much because the crew was so focused. "The tables go into the storage room and chairs get racked so we can roll them in."

Caleb and Grant nodded and headed toward a stack of tables folded against the wall. They each picked up one, but Caleb only made it a few steps before he stopped and set it down. Aaron heard the faintest grunt.

"Caleb?" Grant asked, stopping next to him.

"It's nothing." Caleb picked up the table again and took a couple more steps before he had to stop in obvious discomfort.

Aaron joined them. "It's the foot, isn't it?"

Caleb nodded. "Little bit. I may have stood around too much."

Aaron thought about it, and every time he'd looked over at his table, Caleb had been on his feet. "You should take it easy." Aaron took the table from him. "We don't want your coach coming up here pissed off because you reinjured yourself helping with the school carnival."

Caleb laughed.

"What's so funny about that?" Aaron asked, setting the table down.

"Sorry. I had this image of the team coming up here and marauding through the streets to avenge me."

"Wow," Aaron said, smirking. "You might be a rich and famous athlete, but you've still got that weird imagination."

"This from the guy who played every role-playing game known to man."

"Exactly, so shouldn't I be the one coming up with the marauders?" Aaron could no longer hold back a laugh.

Caleb took the good-natured ribbing with ease. His warm, open smile was disarming, and Aaron felt as if no time at all had passed between them, despite the fact that their lives had taken very different directions over the past fifteen years.

"Maybe Grant should get you home so you can rest?" Aaron eventually said.

"I can...."

"No." Aaron shut down Caleb's protest with the authoritative tone he used with his students. "Just hang tight here, maybe sit down. We'll put these away."

Caleb did as he was told, while Aaron, Grant, and a couple of parents made quick work of the tables and chairs. It was only a few minutes before they returned, and Aaron was in his jacket and had keys out.

"Come on. Let's get outta here," Aaron said.

Caleb cocked his head in disbelief. "Really? Pam's letting you go before she does?"

"You see her over there?" He pointed toward the bleachers against one wall where Pam stood surrounded by a small group. "She's going to be trapped for at least another hour with those parents bending her ear."

As they stepped outside, Aaron braced himself against the crisp evening breeze. Caleb carefully navigated the steps and curb with his cane, following Aaron through the parking lot. Grant jogged ahead to get Caleb's SUV since it was parked farther away.

"So, what brought you back to Foster Grove? If you don't mind me asking?" Caleb asked.

After high school graduation, Aaron had felt the need to

take a few risks and step outside the small-town box he'd always lived in. He'd packed his bags and headed to California. After getting his degree, he'd stayed, found a good teaching position, and was happy—for the most part. "LA kind of... Well, it kind of went bust. Budget cuts slammed down hard, but, luckily, Pam swooped in like my guardian angel and offered me the job here. How about you? What's it like being back after so much time in New York?"

"I love my life, but sometimes you need to escape, know what I mean? I'm enjoying the quiet of being home," Caleb said before leaning in to whisper conspiratorially, "and spending time with old friends. For it being so close, I don't get back nearly enough."

Aaron was struck silent. Caleb's intense gaze left no doubt that he was the old friend Caleb was most interested in spending time with.

"You want to go out sometime?" Caleb asked without breaking eye contact. "Grab dinner or something?"

Aaron deflected the offer because he didn't know what else to do. "Wouldn't you enjoy that more with you sister? Spending time with her, I mean? Give you guys time to catch up?"

"Pam and I talk all the time. I was thinking that you could show me some places that you enjoy or discovered since you've been back in town."

Show him some places?

Aaron didn't know what to say. Caleb's simple invitation sent his brain into overdrive, his thoughts scattering in a thousand different directions. He swallowed, then opened his mouth to answer, but nothing came out. Despite the chill in the air, he felt heat rising in his cheeks and his pulse tick up a notch. Caleb apparently could force him to blush.

A date? With Caleb Carter? Wow.

Wait. Why did he think that? Caleb didn't say date. There was no way Aaron could go on a date with him.

"I mean, we don't have to if you're busy or something." Caleb backpedaled and poked at the pavement with his cane, moving some pebbles around. The crestfallen look on his face was proof that Aaron had let the question hang for too long. "You've probably got papers to grade or a boyfriend to hang out with or something."

Tires crunched on the loose gravel of the parking lot as Grant pulled up. Caleb turned to the passenger-side door and opened it. He tossed his cane inside and, careful of his foot, angled himself to get into the seat.

"I'm single," Aaron offered lamely. "I mean, I don't have a boyfriend. Though my relationship status doesn't really matter, since if we got a bite to eat, we'd be, um, going out as friends."

Caleb flashed that gorgeous smile of his. "Okay, then. Two single friends having a night out. Or at least what passes for a night out in Foster Gove."

What would that even be? Aaron was never good at coming up with things to do.

"Let me think about it. Not the getting-together part," Aaron quickly added before Caleb could misunderstand. "Gotta figure out where to go."

"Cool. I'll pick you up tomorrow night at seven." Caleb got in the SUV. "See you then." He pulled the door closed, lowered the window, and leaned out. "What's your number?" After Aaron recited the number, Caleb entered it, and in a couple of seconds, Aaron's phone rang. "Now we're connected." Caleb raised the window and waved before Grant drove them away.

Aaron stood alone in the elementary school parking lot.

He'd just agreed to go out "as friends" with a man who was the best-looking and one of the most famous players in the entire NHL.

A "friend" whose smile sent Aaron's pulse racing.

He was so screwed.

FIVE

CALEB HAD BEEN LOOKING FORWARD to his friendly date with Aaron all day. He couldn't help but smile as he rounded the street corner and pulled up to the curb where Aaron stood in front of his apartment complex. He wore a sage green sweater and a pair of well-tailored slacks that, despite their conservative style, looked damn sexy on him.

Caleb had spent an inordinate amount of time selecting his wardrobe for the evening. It was important that he looked good, but not like he was trying too hard. He'd chosen a blue pullover and dark jeans, an ensemble that, style-wise, was nearly identical to his date's.

Wait. Totally not a date.

Just two guys having a friendly meal together.

Aaron got into the SUV and buckled his seat belt.

Caleb pulled into traffic and headed toward downtown. "I know part of tonight was for you to show me what you like," he said, "but I thought we might try this new place that Pam took me to the other morning—FG Plate."

"Great. I've had coffee at their café a few times and

JEFF ADAMS & WILL KNAUSS

have always wanted to try the food. I hear their menu is fantastic."

As he drove, Caleb searched his brain for another topic of conversation. He glanced at Aaron in the seat next to him, and all he could think about was how terrific he looked.

"So, how's your foot?" Aaron asked.

"Good. I iced it when I got home and took some ibuprofen. Honestly, today is the best it's felt in weeks. I'm checking in with my physical therapist on Monday, and I'm confident they'll report my recovery is going just as they hoped."

"Happy to hear it. I'm sure the team will be glad to have you back, especially since it means they won't need to maraud their way up here from New York. I didn't want to have to get my armor out of storage."

"Do you really have armor?" Caleb stole a look at Aaron to see if he was serious.

Aaron looked at Caleb and then to the back seat, as if what he was about to say was a secret that needed to be closely guarded. "Maybe."

"Really?"

"It's not like an entire hulking metal thing. It's just some leather armor and chain mail."

Damn. Was he serious? Flashes of Aaron in armor ran through Caleb's imagination. He'd once dated a guy who sometimes asked him to wear his jersey while they were having sex. Aaron dressed as a knight would be very hot, maybe more so if Caleb was in a jersey. Role-play wasn't usually his thing, but this had potential.

"I used to go to renaissance fairs in college," Aaron explained. "I paid a lot of money for it. I keep it for Halloween because the kids seem to love it, plus it's perfect for any parties I might go to because—well, who doesn't like a knight?"

"That's more clever than what I do if I'm pressed into Halloween events."

"Let me guess," Aaron jumped in. "Hockey player?"

"Or hockey coach, which only requires a suit and a dry-erase board with a rink diagram on it." Caleb pulled into the parking lot of FG Plate. "We should do Halloween sometime, and you can be the knight who rescues the hockey player—some sort of a temporal displacement mashup."

"I'm sorry—*temporal displacement mashup*? Did you really say that?"

The idea was ridiculous, but if Caleb was honest, it still sounded fun.

"I've watched enough *Star Trek* to know weird shit can happen with time travel."

Aaron laughed and shook his head. Caleb actually wasn't sure where he wanted things to end up with Aaron, at least from a relationship standpoint. The fact that Aaron seemed relaxed and at ease meant, in Caleb's mind, their evening was off to a pretty good start.

"I hope this is okay." Caleb changed the subject as they got out of the car. "Pam's rarely wrong about food."

"I have no doubt it'll be great. They're all about farm-to-table, getting most of the ingredients from area growers."

"I can't believe you haven't been."

Aaron shook his head and focused on the sidewalk. "Teacher's salary."

Caleb suddenly felt like a dick. He'd assumed since Aaron had lived in LA for so long that he'd made a decent salary, and living in Foster Grove was cheaper than living in most cities on the East Coast. Aaron's cross-country move might have been less about nostalgia for his old hometown and more out of financial necessity. His older car and the aging apartment building he currently called home suggested he might not have money to spare for a night out at a fancy restaurant. Not that any of that mattered to Caleb.

He held the door for Aaron, and they stepped inside FG Plate to find the couple dozen tables at near capacity with a few parties waiting.

"Well, tonight's on me." Caleb stepped up to the host stand before Aaron could argue. "Hi. We've got reservations for two, under Carter."

"Yes, sir." The young host—Caleb guessed she was a high school senior—checked the list. "Yes. Just one moment."

"I can't remember ever needing reservations to eat anywhere in town. Even on the weekend." Caleb returned his attention to Aaron. "It's really changed in the past couple of years. Where it was mostly chain restaurants, now there's all these local places."

"It's a more refined town than when we were growing up. I was shocked when I came back."

"I need to get here more often." As he said it, Caleb realized he meant it. In just the few days he'd been back, he'd surprised himself at how much he enjoyed being back in Foster Grove.

"You should. New York really isn't that far away."

"You sound like Pam or my parents." Caleb smirked at Aaron. "A summer at home with family and friends might be perfect."

The aromas coming from the kitchen were overwhelming in the best way possible. Even though it was spring, the smells might as well have come from a holiday kitchen. *Welcoming* was the word that came to Caleb's mind.

"All right, Mr. Carter. If you'll follow me."

They were seated at a cozy table for two. Despite being at near capacity, the restaurant wasn't overly loud, which would make for easy conversation.

"Here's this evening's menu." The host handed over two planks that had paper secured by twine at the corners. "If you know you want the butterscotch pie for dessert, I recommend preordering. And the apricot pan-seared-scallops appetizer is also moving fast."

"We should definitely start with those scallops. Pie too?" Caleb looked to Aaron.

Aaron's expression said Caleb was crazy for even asking. "For sure."

"Can you please put that in for us?" Caleb smiled at her as he made the request.

"I'd be happy to. Javi will be your server, and he'll be with you in a moment."

After the host left, returning to her post at the front of the restaurant, Caleb focused again on Aaron. "I'm glad we got here before anything sold out. I haven't even read the menu yet, and I already know this is going to be good."

"I don't think it's going to be an easy choice." Aaron's gaze darted across the offerings listed. "It all sounds incredible."

Caleb was stunned as he read the fine print at the bottom of the evening's selections. "No way." He winced at how loud that came out, but he was surprised by what he'd read. "Nate Granger owns this place? And is the chef?"

Aaron laughed as some of the people around them went back to their meals. "New York hockey player makes scene at local restaurant, news at eleven."

Caleb joined in the laughter. "Sorry. But wow. Nate, really?"

"Yeah. You know him?"

"Of course. We were in homeroom together for years."

"That's right. I forgot he was in your class."

Their waiter approached and set two glasses of water on the table.

"Good evening, gentlemen, I'm Javi," the young man said before doing a double take. "Wow, Caleb Carter is at my table. It's a pleasure to meet you."

Caleb nodded. "Nice to meet you, Javi. Rangers fan?"

"No, sir. To be honest, I'm a Sabres guy, but the way you move the puck so smoothly through traffic is incredible."

"Thanks." Caleb smiled, stood, and shook Javi's hand. "I get liking Buffalo. I was the same when I was growing up here. Practically the hometown team."

"Yes, sir. Exactly. We should get on to what you'd like for dinner. I saw that you've ordered an appetizer and dessert. Anything else to start with or just on to the main course?"

"Excuse me, Javi." A man in a burgundy-colored chef's jacket came up behind him. "I had to see if it was true that Caleb Carter was actually in my restaurant."

Caleb smiled. "Nate, good to see you, man." The two shook hands before pulling each other into a back-slapping hug. "I can't believe this place is yours. I thought after graduation you'd be headed off to be some sort of science wizard."

Nate nodded and shrugged. "Two years and I realized I hated it. What I loved was cooking. I cooked for my frat brothers almost every night. I dropped out, pissed off my parents, and went to Paris to study at Le Cordon Bleu.

Bounced around a few restaurants Stateside before I decided to come home and open my own place."

"Congratulations. My sister raves about it. Aaron and I are already having trouble deciding what to order because it all sounds so good. Oh, do you know Aaron Price?"

"Good to see you. Welcome to my place," Nate said, shaking Aaron's hand before turning back to Caleb. "How are you even here? Shouldn't you be playing somewhere?"

"He's injured," Javi chimed in before Caleb could. "He's looking to get back before the first game of the playoffs."

Everyone looked at Javi, surprised.

"What? He's on my fantasy team. It's a thing," he assured them as another server brought out their appetizer.

Nate took their menus. "How about I make the choice easy for you two and put together something special. Some dishes with the very best our kitchen has to offer. If you'd like, I can suggest wine pairings as well."

"I don't want to put you out. You seem busy enough already." Caleb gestured at the full restaurant.

"No trouble at all for an old friend. Make yourselves comfortable, and Javi'll take care of you guys."

"Thanks, Nate."

Caleb sat as Nate retreated to the kitchen, and once Javi went to get the wine Nate suggested for the scallops, they were alone again and wasted no time digging in to the food.

"Seems like he's doing really well for himself."

Aaron nodded as he savored the food. "Another success story for Foster Grove. He's made a real go of it."

Caleb enjoyed the look of pleasure across Aaron's face and tried not fixate on it. He struggled to control a moan as the scallop melted on his tongue. The taste was incredible.

"Does everyone end up coming back here?" Caleb asked once he could speak.

"I don't know about *everyone*. I'm glad I did. I needed the change."

"I figured you'd become, *like, totally* a West Coast guy." Caleb added just a bit of valley speak, which caused Aaron to choke on his water.

"Okay, promise not to do that again." Aaron laughed between a few more coughs. "There was a lot to do in LA, and my parents loved to come out, but...." He shrugged. "It was time to get out. You must think I'm crazy for giving it all up. You love New York, all the people, the excitement?"

"It took me a while to get used to the constant buzz of activity, but I do a lot traveling during the season so I'm not always in the middle of it."

"Now that sounds exhausting," Aaron said as Javi returned with a bottle of wine.

Caleb sampled the pinot gris, which tasted amazing, and Javi poured them each a glass and then left. "I can't complain." Caleb smiled. "I get to play for a living."

"And you have an assistant to do all the stuff you don't want to do."

"I try not to use him as just a gopher. Yes, he makes sure the fridge has food when I come back from the road and that my bills get paid on time. But he also manages my social media, handles appearance requests, coordinates with my agent on the business side of things, and makes sure I don't miss anything I agreed to do."

"He staying up here during your rehab?"

Caleb shook his head. "Grant went back to the city this morning. His boyfriend opens in a play tonight, and I swore I wouldn't let him miss it."

"Sounds like you're a good boss."

44

"I try. It would've been easier on him if I'd stayed in the city. He's fielded a lot of calls about why I left. Does it mean I'm hurt more than I let on? Will it throw my rehab off schedule? It's been worth it, though, since I got to help out the school, see Pam, and reconnect with you."

"Why don't you come home more often, then?"

Caleb considered that while Aaron took another bite of the scallops. "That might be the million-dollar question. It's an easy drive. I could get a place here—either buy something or build new."

Aaron nodded while Caleb finished his scallops just as Javi brought the next course. Nate had outdone himself. Everything placed on their table looked tantalizingly delicious, worthy of a cover on an upscale food magazine. They both eagerly dug in.

"Did you know there are lots for sale near the pond where you played hockey?" Aaron asked between bites of food.

"Really?" Caleb quickly swallowed so he could talk. "A house with a view would be so perfect, especially if I ever had a kid. It'd be cool to—" Caleb stopped and mentally kicked himself.

"What?" Aaron asked when it was clear Caleb wasn't going to continue his train of thought.

"Talking about kids seems, like, I don't know...."

"It's fine. Remember me? Grade school teacher? I like kids. Nothing wrong with saying we both want kids someday." Aaron added a shrug. "Friends can say that to each other."

Friends.

Caleb hoped the evening would mean they might be on the path to be more than that, even though Aaron explicitly said this was not that kind of date.

"Can I ask how is it that you're still single? I've seen pictures of you online with a number of seemingly eligible bachelors."

Caleb rolled his eyes as he finished a bite of roasted lamb. "I do go out occasionally. I'm not a total monk. I've backed off from that recently, though. I'm tired of all the questions about who I'm dating. It's easier—for me and Grant—if I just go solo." Caleb took a drink from his wineglass, which Javi was keeping filled. "As to your actual question, I haven't found the right guy."

Aaron's only response was to nod.

SIX

To AARON'S RELIEF, the conversation flowed easily as topics bounced between hockey, teaching, how Pam still needed to find her Mr. Right, and some of the other ways Foster Grove had changed since high school. They didn't revisit kids or dating—Aaron wasn't going to bring it up, and Caleb had thankfully let it drop.

Earlier, before Caleb stopped by his apartment to pick him up, Aaron had been anxious, unsure of what to expect. But it didn't take long for him to relax and for the evening to feel like dinner with an old friend rather than an internationally famous and devastatingly sexy hockey star.

And Caleb was, without question, sexy. His casually mussed blond hair, shining blue eyes, and muscular body that filled out the light sweater he wore were very appealing.

That was the weird part. He'd always been comfortable around Caleb, but suddenly, it was less like he was Pam's little brother and more like he was a friend. Despite the years since they'd seen each other, something had changed in their dynamic that both excited and, frankly, worried Aaron.

"That was one of the best meals I've ever had," Caleb said as the last of the dinner plates were cleared. "I can't believe this place is in Foster Grove."

"I'm glad you brought me here. It was incredible." Aaron took a last sip of his wine, finishing his glass.

"Ready for dessert?" Javi asked. He'd been an excellent waiter who had an uncanny way of appearing tableside at just the right time all evening. "And maybe some coffee?"

"Can we have dessert in the café? It'd be great to stand for a bit."

"It would be," Aaron agreed. "I feel like I've had more food than a Thanksgiving dinner."

"The chef may have sent too much food." Javi sounded sympathetic. "I can serve you in the café, and you can take as much time as you'd like."

"Coffee now. Pie a little later?" Caleb looked to Aaron.

It was a simple question, but the inquisitive look in Caleb's eyes was stunning and distracting. "Sure."

"I'll get that and meet you over there. Just take any open table."

Javi retreated to the kitchen, and Aaron and Caleb went to the adjoining café. Was it his imagination or were people watching them? It hadn't seemed that way during the meal, but as they moved, Aaron sensed that all eyes were on them. He fought the urge to look around to see how true it was. Did Caleb go through this a lot? If he noticed, he certainly played it cool.

They took one of the bar-height tables and stood together, draping their jackets over the empty stools.

"If the pie wasn't still to come, I'd have suggested a walk," Caleb said, languorously stretching his arms overhead. His sweater pulled up slightly, giving Aaron the briefest glimpse of V-shaped abdominals that tapered below the waist of his tantalizingly low-slung jeans.

Aaron quickly looked away and mentally chided himself.

Walking with Caleb on an evening like tonight sounded nice, but what Aaron was thinking about drifted into date territory. What game was he playing with himself? There was no way he was ready to date, and even if he were, he knew he wasn't right for Caleb.

Javi brought coffee and told them he'd check back. He'd barely gone when a hand came down on Caleb's shoulder.

"Caleb Carter." The voice was loud, booming, causing several of the café's patrons to turn, and even Caleb flinched. "I didn't expect to run into you here."

Caleb looked to his side and smiled, recovering from the surprise. "Rick Hargrove. Great to see you." The two bumped fists.

Aaron knew Rick coached one of the town's peewee hockey teams and was a former teammate of Caleb's, going all the way back to middle school. Rick was a typical jock, had been as long as Aaron had known him. Seeing Caleb in comparison, it was like Caleb wasn't a jock at all. Where Rick seemed to want to fill the room with his personality, Caleb's quiet confidence appealed more to Aaron.

"Aaron, do you know Rick?"

"Of course. Rick, good to see you."

"Price." He nodded briefly in Aaron's direction but then returned his full attention to Caleb. "I couldn't get to the carnival last night, so it's dumb luck to run into you here. What are you up to?"

"Having dinner and catching up." Caleb looked around Rick and raised his eyebrows at Aaron.

"You should come over. We could watch a game or two," Rick continued, as if he hadn't heard Caleb's answer and was unable to decipher the hint that he might be a third wheel. "We could watch any team you want."

"He's actually avoiding games." It wasn't Aaron's usual style to interrupt, but he didn't like the vibe between Rick and Caleb. "He's anxious enough about not being able to play."

"Yeah. I'm only watching what Coach tells me to so I can stay up on strategy. You know how it feels to be scratched."

"Sure do. I had that broken arm our sophomore year and was out the last half of the season. Tell you what. Why don't you come help me coach instead? My team would love to see you."

"I'm not skating quite yet, so...."

"No matter. You can coach from the bench. Price here can come along. We always need more adults to help corral the players."

Aaron was surprised by the invitation. He knew how to skate, sure, but he wasn't exactly known for his athletic prowess. Although if it meant he'd get to hang out with Caleb more, he'd consider it. But coaching? He wasn't so sure. And was corralling players an actual hockey term?

"How's the team this year?" Caleb asked as Aaron considered a graceful way of turning the offer down.

"It's a good batch of kids. Third in the division right now and looking to step it up before playoffs."

"All right. I'll bring some plays, and we'll see what I can do to help push that. Can you help get me some solo ice time? I need to get back on skates next week, and I haven't heard back from anyone at the rink about scheduling it."

"I can get that set up later tonight. I'll email the slots I schedule you for." Rick tore his gaze away from Caleb to look at Aaron. "You in for coaching, Price? You can skate, right?"

"Of course I can," he said, with a little too much pride in his voice. "Just say when."

"Great! See you both Monday afternoon at four thirty." Rick gave Caleb a hug and went to the counter.

Had those two ever been a thing? Aaron could've been reading the situation completely wrong, but it felt like they might have been more than just teammates. As far as he knew, Caleb hadn't come out until college, just like he'd done, but that didn't mean there wasn't something going on secretly before that.

"He hasn't changed at all." Caleb sighed and looked to Aaron. "Sorry about that."

"It's okay. I remember what he was like in school."

Caleb took a sip of his coffee. "You didn't have to agree to help with coaching."

Aaron shrugged in a way he hoped conveyed nonchalance, but all he managed to do was knock the handle of his coffee mug with the back of his hand, sending a portion of its contents across the table. Luckily, it was a small spill, and he mopped it up quickly with some napkins. "It'll be cool to see you in your element. Did you always know you wanted to play pro?"

"Oh yeah. High school was all about getting into a college with a good program where I could get noticed. Don't get me wrong—the education was important too, you know, in case I didn't make it to the pros. I admit, I'd been worried about bailing my senior year, but I wasn't going to pass on my chance to get into the draft."

"I thought you finished college? I could swear Pam told

me you had a degree in... Oh, what was it?" Aaron searched his mind for the missing detail.

"Communications." Caleb's smile warmed Aaron far more than the coffee. "I split my senior year between online and summer school. It took a couple years to get it done, but I finished."

Aaron studied Caleb further. He was full of surprises. Sticking with school while he was a rookie was impressive, and even more so because he likely could've finished much later.

"My turn." Caleb broke into Aaron's thoughts. "Always wanted to be a teacher?"

"Ever since I was tutoring in high school. That moment when someone connects with the information is so fulfilling. I get to do that every day, and I love it."

"Just like you did with me." Aaron tingled as Caleb spoke softly. "I'd love to come watch you teach some time."

"Really?" Sure, he had people sit in on his classes from time to time, but why would Caleb what to do that? Would Aaron even be able to concentrate with him there, or would he be stuck stammering? "It's not exactly a spectator sport."

"Well, you're going to see my teaching skills, of a sort, in action. I should get to see yours, no?"

"I suppose. Would you be willing to talk to the class about what it's like being a pro athlete?"

"Hey, now, don't try to change what this is about." Caleb bumped his shoulder against Aaron's. "I want to see how you do it."

Aaron recovered quickly, even though the brief touch from Caleb had sent a wave of excitement through him. "Yeah, but if you don't talk to the class, they're not going to pay attention since there'd be a celebrity in the back of the room."

Caleb cocked his head and looked at Aaron as if weighing carefully what he'd heard. "Okay. I don't want to be a disruption." Caleb's dazzling smile nearly destroyed Aaron's composure because it was breathtaking. "Name the day and I'll give some sort of career-day-type spiel, and then I'll watch you do your thing."

"I'll look over the plans for next week and let you know what day's good."

Caleb gave a sharp nod. "Perfect. Say, what do you think about getting the pie to go and taking that stroll?"

"Good idea."

"We can get to the part of the evening where you show me all the new sights of our bustling little metropolis."

There was plenty he could show Caleb in this neighborhood. "Of course. I'd love to get a place in this part of town one day, so I know the area pretty well."

"Great."

They flagged down Javi, who quickly had their dessert ready to take with them. "Here's the pie," he said, handing them a bag with the restaurant's tasteful logo stamped on the side. "The chef said that tonight was his treat, and, if you're not too busy, he'd love to get together while you're in town."

"Please tell Nate thank you and that it was superb. And I'll give him a call." Caleb pulled out his wallet and removed some bills. "Thank you, Javi, for taking such good care of us."

Javi took the cash and looked at it with wide eyes. "Thank you, that's very generous. I'll make sure this gets into the tip pool for tonight."

Caleb smiled, looking extremely pleased. "Have a good night." He clapped Javi on the shoulder before turning to Aaron. "Let's walk."

SEVEN

Caleb worried that Aaron wasn't having a good time. The evening was supposed to just be two people catching up. Yes, Caleb found Aaron more attractive than ever, and he'd love the chance to take things further. But he wouldn't risk the renewed friendship, or Pam's wrath, just to get what he'd wanted since he was sixteen. So far, Aaron hadn't seemed interested in going down that path.

"You sure this walk's a good idea?" Even as he asked, Aaron led them away from where the SUV was parked and down a sidewalk filled with storefronts.

"If my foot acts up, I'll let you know," Caleb said as he looked at the buildings around them. "This area has really transformed. Pam said there'd been changes, but this is quite impressive."

"Most of it's happened in the last year. Nate moving in and updating the look of the building before he opened has a lot to do with it, from what I've heard. New places are still popping up in this area too."

"I remember when hardly anything was open after seven, even on the weekends." Caleb traded nods with the people who acknowledged him. "It's weird seeing all this activity and it's almost nine."

"Pam and I spent many weekend nights sitting in the same booth at Denny's because it was the only place open late."

Caleb enjoyed the trip down memory lane. Denny's was the place he and his teammates would go after hockey games because it could easily accommodate a couple dozen hungry teenagers. "It still around?"

"Oh yeah. Most of the new places are too expensive for the high school crowd, so they still end up there."

"It'd be fun to get Pam and hang out in your old booth." Caleb laughed at his idea. "If you'd let me, that is. You two never wanted me to hang around there."

"You were a junior and her brother. It just wasn't right." Aaron became more animated and Caleb liked it. It was the freest Aaron had been all evening. "As the local sports star, I think you'd decide who could sit with you. And I'm sorry to say, our booth is gone. They remodeled, and that side of the restaurant is all freestanding tables and chairs."

"I can't believe Pam let them do that."

"Right. Although she blames me since I wasn't here to help stop it." Aaron's mood faltered. Caleb knew Pam would've only meant that as a joke, so the reaction was strange. "Sometimes she acts like I didn't miss her because I didn't visit, but it just never worked out."

"What's important is you're back now. One day she won't hold that over your head. Either that, or you could try to get Denny's to put her booth back."

Aaron laughed so hard he snorted, and Caleb's heart soared. Whatever funk had threatened had been pushed aside.

"Oh, this is nice," Aaron said, stopping to look in a storefront window. "We were just talking about this."

The large oil painting captivated Caleb. Broad, vibrant brush strokes depicted the woods and pond he and his friends had played on every winter before they'd gone their separate ways. The perspective was looking through trees, with the ice and players in the distance. Tree branches were bare except for a few evergreens, and snow covered the ground while the slate-gray sky hinted that more snow was on the way. He was transported back some twenty years, as if the painter had been a voyeur during one of Caleb's many afternoons there.

"It's beautiful," Aaron said, standing close to Caleb.

Caleb said nothing, lost in the painting and the memories it conjured. He didn't know art, didn't know how to describe why this picture pulled on him. There were photos of him at the pond, some with a similar point of view, but they didn't capture the feelings this did.

"I might need to come back when the artist is here," he said quietly. "It's really breathtaking." He gazed at it for a few more moments before his attention drifted to Aaron's soft smile reflected in the glass. The way the corner of Aaron's mouth quirked up into a slightly lopsided grin caused butterflies to churn in Caleb's stomach. It was so damn sweet. "Sorry. I didn't mean to get carried away."

"Don't apologize. It's a gorgeous painting. I'm sure the artist would love to know your reaction," Aaron said, putting his hand on Caleb's shoulder before quickly removing it.

The gesture implied a casual intimacy. Something Caleb didn't mind at all, but Aaron obviously didn't feel was appropriate for two friends out for a casual stroll.

"Kids still play on that pond, right?" he asked.

"Of course. They were out there all the time last winter, even during snowstorms."

"That's the best time to play." Caleb tore himself away from the window, and they meandered along the sidewalk. "It snowed during the outdoor game the Rangers played in a couple of years ago. You'd swear all the players had become ten years old again. Both teams had a blast and wanted it to go to overtime so we could keep going."

"I watched that. It looked fun, but, man, the people in the stands looked cold."

"It helps to stay moving and to have heaters on the bench," Caleb said with a wink.

It was hard in moments like this to forget this wasn't a date. It was a wonderful evening and the best nongame night Caleb could remember in a while. So many feelings had flooded him when Aaron had put his hand on his shoulder for that brief moment. He wasn't sure what had spooked Aaron, but he wished for the contact again.

What would dating Aaron be like? Caleb had fantasies about it in high school. He'd envisioned Aaron asking him to prom. He'd seen Aaron in his tux that spring, and the image was seared into his brain—even more than a decade later, he could conjure it up. There'd also been a dream where Aaron took him to Homecoming, and they ended the night making out under the bleachers.

As they walked, Caleb continually fought the urge to hold Aaron's hand. The street gradually turned from storefronts to houses. Caleb had always liked this part of town, with its slightly older homes that usually had a lot of character. His parents' house was in a cookie-cutter-type neighborhood, and while they were nice houses, they just weren't that interesting. It was nice that the artsy, revitalized part of downtown they'd just passed through led right to these older homes.

Aaron suddenly stopped. "No way."

They stood at an intersection, and to their right was a smallish house, which, other than a mowed lawn and trimmed landscape, hadn't seen much upkeep. There was a For Sale sign in the yard with a notice that the price was newly reduced. It was a corner lot, which provided a large front and side yard. Caleb thought the word *cottage* would best describe the house since it took up only about a quarter of the available space.

Aaron went across the lawn to the sign and pulled out an information sheet from the plastic holder. He groaned as Caleb approached.

"What's wrong?"

"I've been hoping this place would drop in price, but it's still out of my price range," he said, showing Caleb the new list price. "It came on the market six months ago. I'd love to refurbish it. It'd be so cute. Imagine all the trim and shutters a pristine white, and the cedar shake siding back to its darkish red color."

"You've thought a lot about this." Caleb loved the dreamy look in Aaron's eyes and the passion in his voice.

"Yeah." Aaron furrowed his brows in disappointment. "I know that one day I'm going to come by here and the word *Sold* will be across this sign."

"What's it like inside?" Caleb asked, wanting to hear more about this place that captivated Aaron.

Aaron grinned broadly. "It's trapped in the fifties and sixties. It needs work desperately. But even as is, it's cute." He looked wishful, as if considering the possibilities. "I wouldn't make it all modern—some of that fifties Cape Cod style is what I like—but the kitchen cries out for updated appliances, and the floors need a lot of love."

Caleb grinned as Aaron went on.

"Two bedrooms, including one that takes up most of the upstairs. There's a garage around back. And this yard... Can you imagine what could be done out here?" Aaron spread his arms wide to encompass the space, and Caleb could easily see many things that would make it incredible.

"Have you put in an offer?"

"I haven't had the nerve," he said, stepping away from the fence and seeming to come back to reality. "It really is out of my price range."

It was a nice house, and even in its current condition, it looked solid. Aaron's vision appealed to Caleb. While his loft in the city was well-appointed, even before making this trip home, he'd often considered getting a house outside the city that was simpler, more cozy. It seemed Aaron was going for that feeling too.

"Come on. Let's go before I decide to break in and become a squatter." Aaron laughed as he said it, but there was a tinge of regret too.

Caleb was seeing a whole new side of Aaron, and it made him want to know even more. It wouldn't be a completely bad idea to spend the off-season in Foster Grove.

Even as he rolled these thoughts over, Caleb recognized the feelings that were rising up after a long dormancy. He was crushing on Aaron Price, just like he always had.

EIGHT

Aaron had dreaded this afternoon since he'd gotten home Saturday night and thought about what he'd committed to. He could handle seeing Caleb again. Saturday had been amazing, but he wasn't going to date Caleb. So why did he care if Rick was on the hunt? There wasn't an answer—other than he did care.

Aaron went straight to the rink from school because he wanted to arrive before practice to get laced up and comfortable on his skates. It hadn't been a lie that he knew how to skate; it'd just been a few years. He hoped walking around the lobby for fifteen minutes would help remind him what it felt like to be in skates and get him ready for the ice. As he paced, players, already dressed for practice, arrived with their parents. Aaron liked seeing that when Caleb strolled into Wonderland Ice Palace, he didn't have the cane. It took only a moment before he was surrounded by kids excited to see him. It took Rick blowing his whistle to remind the kids to finish preparing for practice.

Whatever vibe there'd been between Caleb and Rick at

the café wasn't there. It was stupid to think it would be. This wasn't the place for it.

Rick called Aaron over to where he stood with two other adults who were also on skates. Rick introduced him to Ian and Kelly. "Thanks to Aaron for joining our volunteer ranks this afternoon. Caleb's going to take the team through plays and drill, and it'll be more important than ever that you three make sure the players are on point and paying attention. I'll split you up among the different groups, and as always, you'll help move barriers and cones to keep practice running smooth."

Rick blew his whistle again and announced it was time to hit the ice. Kids stampeded toward the entrance. Aaron and the other assistants followed the trail of eight- and nine-year-olds from the lobby to the rink.

"It's good to see you." Caleb fell in step next to Aaron, who concentrated on how he was walking. "How was the rest of your weekend?"

Aaron's heart got fluttery with Caleb next to him. "Busy, but good. Had to grade a test and review book report outlines."

"Oh man, I hated outlines." Caleb visibly shuddered, and Aaron didn't know if it was from the chill in the air or the memory of the school work.

"Everyone does." Aaron chuckled. "We learn in Teacher 101 that it's an ideal way to irritate students."

"Somehow I wouldn't be surprised if that's true. Just like how coaches use suicide drills to frustrate and exhaust. So, you ready for this?" Caleb seemed energized and ready to tackle the practice session.

"I think so. It's a different way to spend an afternoon," Aaron said, trying and failing to match Caleb's enthusiasm.

"Wanna grab dinner after?"

That wasn't going to make it easier to keep from getting too involved. After the amazing Saturday night, Aaron needed to keep some distance between them, otherwise his heart would send him down a slippery slope.

"Sure. I'd love to." The words tumbled out of Aaron's mouth before he could stop them. What was he thinking? Which part of his brain pushed the button to allow him to say that?

"Great."

They were at the door to the rink when Caleb grabbed Aaron's arm and prevented him from stepping on the ice.

"What's wrong?" Aaron looked at Caleb, who kept a firm grip to prevent him from going forward. Everyone else was on the ice, and he didn't want it to look like he was shirking his responsibilities.

Caleb gestured down with his eyes, and Aaron followed the gaze.

Oh crap. The skate guards were still on.

"Thanks," Aaron said as he took off the plastic blade protectors. Caleb maintained his hold to help him balance as he lifted each foot to get the guards. "That would've been embarrassing."

"Everyone does it. I've had more than a few falls because I forgot about them."

Once Aaron put the guards on the small ledge that ran around the boards, Caleb released him, and Aaron wished he could do something else that would require him to grab on again.

"Well, thanks for saving me." Aaron looked for an escape before he did or said something else wrong. "I'm going to go help get those cones in place."

Aaron took off. He didn't fall, but he moved with caution and a lack of speed he didn't see in the other assis-

JEFF ADAMS & WILL KNAUSS

tants. It was painfully obvious he hadn't skated in some time.

Caleb walked—or sort of slid—across the ice to one of the benches. Aaron didn't know how he navigated the ice in his sneakers so easily. The players, meanwhile, didn't get in Caleb's way as they did their warmups, skating around the cones and following Rick's orders on when to change direction.

Caleb and Rick talked at the bench as Aaron and Ian watched the skaters do the drills. Sometimes Ian would call out to speed it up. More and more Aaron's focus drifted from the players around him to the conversation at the bench. As he watched, Caleb occasionally moved his dry-erase pen over the small whiteboard he had with the diagram of the rink on it, although he wasn't actually writing on it. When the two broke out laughing, Aaron tried to squash the pang of jealously at not being in on whatever was funny.

The whistle blew again. The players gathered at the bench and the assistants cleared the cones off the ice. Aaron had trouble moving the cones because they threw off his balance, and it pissed him off that he was looking bad in front of Caleb.

Over the next ninety minutes, Aaron felt ridiculous as he skated around poorly, doing what he needed to. He hated that Ian had to help him clear his part of the ice. He was sure he was being ridiculed by the players too. He imagined Caleb wanting to distance himself from such a bad skater. What had he been thinking when he'd thought he'd be able to manage this job?

Aaron tried to focus on the enjoyment of watching Caleb. His interaction with the players was delightful. He diagrammed plays, took questions, and always remained calm. He only yelled to be heard across the rink, and it was easy to tell he wasn't angry—unlike Rick, who yelled in frustration a lot. At one point, Aaron was sure Caleb even chastised Rick for that.

His favorite moment was when Caleb came off the bench to work with a player having trouble with a slap shot. Caleb showed him some techniques and shot with him a few times. His message to the team was: When you see someone having trouble with a skill you can do, help them out. Don't leave them to struggle, and never taunt. Teamwork was working with each other—all the time.

Aaron was proud of Caleb as he saw signs of recognition and understanding among some of the players. Caleb was a good teacher, or in this case, coach.

Once practice ended and the kids dispersed, Aaron helped pick up the pucks so the Zamboni could clean the ice. Caleb was crossing the ice with Rick as Aaron came up to them.

"Nice job with the coaching, Caleb," Aaron said, trying and failing to slow down, much less stop.

Caleb reached out with quick reflexes and steadied him. "Careful."

"You really should learn to skate better if you're going to help," Rick said.

Aaron tried to keep from shooting daggers with his eyes.

"What did we just learn about teamwork?" Caleb looked to Rick as he kept his arm out for Aaron to use to stay steady as they moved to the door to exit the ice. Aaron loved the teacherlike positive quality in Caleb's voice, rather than a condescending one.

"Point taken." Rick didn't sound completely convinced of that. "Thanks for helping out, Price."

As they stepped off the rink, Caleb rolled his eyes at

Aaron, who gave a weak smile, before he talked with some of the players around him. A couple of parents pulled Rick away as Aaron sat on the bleachers to get out of his skates. He was in way over his head with this and just wanted to go home—except he'd agreed to hang out with Caleb. That was going to be a nightmare. Caleb had to be embarrassed about Aaron's performance today even if he had just defended him to Rick.

Caleb broke away from the group as parents tried to corral their kids to get changed. He was almost to Aaron as one more player intercepted him.

"Mr. Carter? Can you show us more stuff?"

"That's up to Coach Rick."

Rick turned as he heard his name. The young player saw that as his opportunity. "Coach, can Mr. Carter come back?"

"If he's got the time, yes."

"When are you on the ice next?"

"Wednesday and Friday before our game on Saturday," the player said.

"I can make that." Caleb didn't miss a beat, and the players cheered in response.

"Thanks, man." Rick clapped Caleb on the back. "You've got a knack for this. You want to grab a drink or something and have that catch-up?"

Maybe this was Aaron's out. Caleb would surely go with Rick.

"I'll have to take a rain check on that. I've already got a date." Caleb stole a look at Aaron, who quickly looked away, shocked at what he'd heard.

Date? He actually said *date*. There were other terms he could've used, even a simple *I'm hanging out with Aaron*. There couldn't be *dates*. He knew he didn't fit with Caleb at

66

all—except he sort of did. Sometimes. Maybe just not here. The conflicting thoughts drove Aaron crazy.

"Fair enough. Maybe some other time, then?"

Unless Aaron was misreading, Rick was flirting a bit, just like the other night. Although Aaron might not be in the best position to judge.

"We'll see." Caleb turned away from Rick and sat next to Aaron.

Before Caleb could say anything, Ian joined them. "If you're coming back on Wednesday, text me." He handed over a card. "You don't need much skating work. I'd be happy to help out ahead of practice."

"Thanks. I appreciate that." Aaron smiled and stood to shake Ian's hand.

"My pleasure. It's great having someone else out there to keep practice moving for the kids."

"Yeah, thanks." Caleb stood too. "I was planning to coach him as well since I've got ice time right before practice Wednesday." Caleb turned to Aaron. "With two of us working with you, you'll be whipped into shape in no time."

Suddenly, he had two people helping him. He didn't know what to say to that.

A player came up to Ian, dragging a huge bag behind him. "You ready, Bobby?" Ian asked.

He nodded.

"All right. I'll see you Wednesday."

Bobby gave a small wave to Caleb, who returned it before they walked away.

"Shall we?" Caleb looked at Aaron.

"Yeah." He picked up his skate bag.

"You really didn't do bad today. Ian's right—you just need a brush up. Rick was just being a jerk. He was like that when we were teammates back in high school. I was glad to see he doesn't teach that to the kids, but I didn't appreciate him tearing you down."

"I think he's trying to impress you."

Caleb nodded as they headed out to the parking lot. "I know. He's tried over the years to get me interested. He was out before I was, and as soon as word got to him that I'd finally done it, he emailed saying we should get together. He's a friend, for sure, but there are aspects to his personality that don't make him boyfriend material—things like tearing people down."

Aaron fought the urge to take Caleb's hand as those warm feelings rose up inside him yet again. He really needed to find a way to keep those at bay—because he wasn't boyfriend material either.

NINE

I'm cleared for skating.
Celebrate with me tonight?
My house. Dinner. At 6.

Caleb pressed send before he could think too much about it. It was an excruciating seventeen minutes before a message came back.

Congrats. Dinner it is. What can I bring?

Yes! Aaron agreed to another get-together. That would be three days out of four—or five if he counted the evening of the carnival—that he got to hang out with him.

His grocery trip was interesting because the citizens of Foster Grove weren't expecting to find Caleb pushing a cart through the local market in the middle of the afternoon. There were more than a few stares, which he found funny. Caleb simply nodded and smiled at those who gawked.

In the pasta aisle, he thought the stock boy who was putting sale tags on some of the noodles might get a crick in his neck as he kept turning to look at Caleb while he surveyed the selection. When he dropped his tags, Caleb kneeled to pick up the ones that fluttered to the floor at his feet.

"Oh my God. I'm so sorry." Caleb saw the guy's name was Liam. He looked around, as if fearing who might have seen his fumble.

"No problem." He handed over what he'd collected.

"Thank you, Mr. Carter," he said nervously.

"It's Caleb."

"I can't believe you're here. I wanted to meet you at the carnival, but I couldn't get off work that night."

"Pleasure to meet you, Liam."

"How'd you know my—?" Caleb smiled and subtly gestured at Liam's shirt. "Oh, right. I'm not usually so scattered. It's so cool to meet you. I play center at the high school just like you did."

"Always good to meet a fellow center. Are you having a good season?"

"I'm sorry, Mr. Carter, is Liam bothering you?"

Caleb watched Liam go pale as he saw who was behind him.

Caleb turned to find a stern-looking woman in a pantsuit wearing a name tag that read *Gloria* with *Manager* underneath. "Not at all, ma'am. He was helping me pick out some spaghetti, and we got to talking." Caleb turned on some charm. There was no need for Liam to get into trouble.

"All right. If you're sure." She eyed Liam. "We don't want our employees disturbing the customers."

"He wasn't. We're just two hockey players bonding over noodles. I promise."

She nodded, still not looking satisfied. "Get those tags done as soon as you're finished assisting Mr. Carter. There's stock to unload in the back."

"Yes, ma'am," Liam said. "So, Mr. Carter," he said as he pulled a box of spaghetti off the shelf, "this is what my mom uses all the time, and it's on sale."

Caleb nodded. "Is she gone?" he whispered, and Liam nodded. "Good. She's kinda scary."

"Yes, she is." Liam gave a lopsided smile.

"Thanks for the recommendation." He took the box and added it to his cart. "I'll leave you to your work. I don't want her coming back for you."

Liam held out his fist, and Caleb bumped it. "Thanks, Mr.—I mean, Caleb. Thanks, Caleb."

A few aisles over, Caleb ended up signing a few autographs for some shoppers, the majority of which were on blue Powerade bottles since that was the drink he'd endorsed a few years back. He grabbed an extra bottle and dropped it in his cart as well. Once he'd paid, he went looking for Liam, who was in the dairy section stocking bags of shredded cheese.

"Hey," he said, looking around.

"Um, hey," Liam said, sounding confused.

"Got a marker on you?" Caleb spoke softly.

"Yeah." Liam pulled a black pen from his pants pocket.

"Perfect." Caleb set his bags down, pulled out the Powerade bottle he'd bought, and signed it. "Here you go. It was nice meeting you."

He handed the bottle and the pen to Liam, whose mouth hung open.

"This is the coolest thing ever. The guys aren't going to believe this." Liam put his fist out for another bump, which Caleb happily met. "Thanks, Caleb."

"You're welcome. See you around."

Caleb gathered up his bags, and he and Liam nodded to each other.

He'd picked up ingredients for something he knew he could make—spaghetti with meatballs. No way was he going to try a new dish for the first time with Aaron. It was risky enough cooking for him since they'd eaten at Nate's restaurant—Caleb's food was in no way comparable to that.

Shortly before six, Caleb put the al dente spaghetti into the sauce, splattering it all over the stovetop and nearby counter. "Dammit," he said softly as he stirred the pasta. He was more careful with dropping in the meatballs he'd already partially cooked.

The doorbell rang as he got the final meatball settled. He stole a look at the clock on the stove. "Of course he's on time. Just like I would be. Stupid sauce." The cleanup would have to wait. At least none of the sauce made it to his light blue shirt.

At the door, Caleb's breath hitched as he saw Aaron through the beveled glass panels. Aaron looked sharp in black jeans and a light purple button-down with a coordinating tie and tailored jacket. Caleb was going to see Aaron in his classroom tomorrow, and if he dressed like this, it would be very difficult to focus on his teaching rather than how attractive he looked.

He opened the door. "Hey. Come on in."

"Sorry," Aaron said, sounding flustered as he stepped inside. "I'd hoped to be early to help with the cooking, but I got stuck talking to your sister about some students. I did pick up pie from Nate's, though." He held up a shopping bag.

"Don't be silly. You're right on time—and even if you weren't, you brought pie and that makes up for practically anything." Caleb quickly embraced Aaron to say hello. It was involuntary, and even surprised him. He liked how Aaron felt, perfectly huggable, with just enough firmness to feel sturdy but enough mushiness to be snuggly. He wished he could've held on longer. One day, maybe, Aaron would feel comfortable enough to fully hug him back. "Trouble today?"

"Nothing out of the ordinary. It's a constant battle to keep the bullying at bay and to try to turn it around. One of the usual suspects acted out, and there were reports to file and a meeting after school."

"Well, you're here now, and there are no misbehaving kids."

"Thank God. If you were harboring any, I'd have to take action on that, and I'd really rather not."

They both laughed as Aaron hung up his jacket on one of the hooks just inside the door. Caleb was mesmerized. This was only work attire, but everything fit just right and gave Caleb an idea of what might be under the clothes.

"Come on back to the kitchen. I'm finishing up."

As they walked to the back of the house, Caleb's phone rang. He pulled it from his pocket with the intention of silencing it until he saw who it was.

"I should take this. It'll only be a minute. Make yourself at home."

Aaron nodded and went on to the kitchen while Caleb turned back to the living room.

"Hey, Phil. This—"

"Caleb, what are you trying to do to us?" His agent never was one for small talk. "You've been cleared to skate, and yet you're still up there relaxing with your hometown crowd. And I've seen pictures of you on ice with kids. What's going on?"

"If you know I'm cleared to skate, you know that happened, like, three hours ago. As for the kids, I'm helping out a friend who coaches a local team. I'd think you'd love that kind of publicity."

"Not while you're supposed to be injured! If you're going to do that kind of stuff, you should do it here so local TV can cover it, not in some small town no one cares about. You know what you do in the media is even more important with the upcoming contract negotiations."

"Important to you or to the team?" Caleb tried not to get frustrated since Phil worked for his best interests, but he wasn't in the mood for a lecture. "I've got more than a decade in New York. If they wanted me to be in the city, I'd be—"

"It's perception, Caleb. You've done this long enough—"

"I'm not having this conversation right now. I'll call you tomorrow." He disconnected before Phil could piss him off further, then put the phone on silent. He took a deep breath before he returned to the kitchen, where he found Aaron sitting at the island. "Sorry about that."

"That was bubbling and sending sauce onto the stove," Aaron said, pointing to Caleb's workstation, "so I stirred it and cleaned up."

"You didn't have to do that. Most of it splattered before you got here."

"Not a problem. It's the least I can do for the meal."

Caleb checked the pot before turning quickly back to Aaron. "I'm an awful host. Would you like something to drink?"

"No, I'm good."

"I've got a great wine to go with dinner. We'll be ready in just a few minutes."

"I'm impressed with all the work your parents did on the house."

Caleb opened the oven and pulled out the garlic bread. "They renovated right after they retired, and this was their biggest project. I don't think they even use the living room anymore. They usually just sit where you are and do whatever, especially since they put the TV in." Caleb indicated the screen mounted to the wall with a pivot so it could be seen from the adjacent dining room or anywhere in the kitchen. "Or they just sit on the deck," he said as he transferred the bread into a serving basket, "where they essentially built a second living room."

"Where are they, anyway? On the way here, I was trying to remember the last time I'd seen them in town."

"Let's see. Today I think they're in Rome." Caleb picked his phone up from the counter and flipped through some screens. "Yup, Rome today and tomorrow. They're doing an around-the-world trip."

"That's a bucket-list thing for me. They're having a good retirement, I hope."

"Oh yes. They've even learned how to use Facebook Live to show Pam and me things in real time."

"You set all that up for them, didn't you?"

"Yeah. They gave us a lot growing up, and I was in a position to help them do anything they wanted. Redo the house. Go on a trip. Whatever." The timer dinged, and Caleb pulled the pot off the stove and carefully emptied the contents into a large bowl. "Dinner's ready. We can eat here, in the dining room, or outside."

"Outside? Really?" Aaron sounded dubious. "It's nice out, but a little chilly."

"Trust me. I can fix that. Just follow me." Caleb took the big bowl of steaming pasta and the garlic bread.

"I'll grab these." Aaron took the plates, napkins, glasses, and utensils from the counter and followed. He stopped just outside the door to the deck. "Whoa. This is nice."

"Hang on." Caleb set the food down on the table and returned to flip some switches on a panel by the door. Two heaters turned on, a waterfall activated farther away, and outdoor lighting illuminated the entire yard.

"Dang," Aaron said.

"They wanted to extend spring and fall just a bit. Be right back. Just need the wine." Caleb darted back inside.

When he returned, Aaron had set up places on the table. Caleb watched from behind as Aaron served the food. Was this what life could be like if he settled down with someone—really took the time to find the right person and build a life? A simple weekday meal on the back deck, home-cooked, winding down at the end of the day.

Aaron suddenly turned. "Everything okay?"

"I just... nothing. It was silly."

"If you say so." Aaron studied Caleb closely for another minute, leaving him feeling very exposed. It wasn't like Aaron could see what he was thinking, but it sure felt like he was trying to.

"Hope you like pinot noir. I think it's the best thing to go with this dish."

"Works for me." Aaron sat, and Caleb took the adjacent seat, where Aaron had put the other place setting. He poured a generous glass for each of them.

"Cheers," Caleb said, raising his glass.

Aaron clinked his glass against Caleb's. "Cheers. To old acquaintances."

"Just acquaintances?"

He watched as Aaron took a moment to thoughtfully reconsider.

"How about," Aaron offered, "old friends becoming reacquainted?"

"I like the sound of that."

They toasted again and each took a drink before they dug into the meal. "This is delicious," Aaron finally said between bites.

"Glad you like it. It's certainly nothing like Nate's food, but what I lack in culinary expertise I more than make up in... I don't know, enthusiasm, I guess."

"Well, I enthusiastically declare this meal a success. Do you cook often?"

"On days I'm home and it's not game day. Those are too busy, and on the road, it's impossible to."

"Me too. I cook a lot because it's affordable. Plus, I like to bring my lunch because I can't stand cafeteria food."

"I have to say," Caleb said, focusing on Aaron, "you look very handsome tonight. The shirt, the tie—it's a great look."

"Oh, thanks." Caleb's compliment seemed to leave Aaron momentarily flustered. Aaron set his fork down and picked up his napkin, absently wiping at the corner of his mouth. "I can be more casual, but I kind of like dressing like this. And it shows the students a good, professional look too. You spiff up really well. I've seen those suits you wear to the arena."

"I love that you still follow hockey," Caleb said, smiling as he held Aaron's gaze. "I would've never suspected it."

"It's your fault, you know."

"Pam's the one who dragged you to games not—"

"Right, when her boyfriends had some other sporty thing to do. Then I caught on that I could explain some of the geometry based on how the puck moved. By the time I graduated, I was hooked."

Caleb refilled their wineglasses. So far, the meal had

gone well. Good conversation, good food, great company. "And that helped my game too. The way you taught that helped me see new patterns—not only how the puck moved, but players too, and how I could intercept them."

"See, math can be used after you graduate." Aaron took a bite of garlic bread and then made a sound of realization, which caused him to chew faster so he could talk. "Since you're coming to observe tomorrow, why don't you help me teach? It won't be actual geometry, of course, but we could talk about basic shapes and principles and connect it to hockey. The kids would love that."

Caleb nodded. "Sure. But if you're going to make me state any theorems or something, you'd better be offering a refresher course."

"I promise I won't put the hockey player on the spot."

Aaron looked excited, and it was an expression Caleb wanted to see more often. His instincts said to lean over and kiss Aaron, but that wouldn't be right. As much as he wanted a date, a real date, he had to settle for the friendly get-togethers. But the more time they spent in each other's company, the more Caleb wanted to move to that level. But he needed some signal from Aaron that it'd be okay.

Instead, Caleb moved to safer topics. "Since I'm back on skates tomorrow, I have an idea. How about we skate together after school? I watch you teach, and then I coach you."

"Okay," Aaron said without a pause to even think about it.

"I'll do my rehab workout in the morning, join you for the second half of the school day, and then we have skating school and on to team practice?"

"It's a—I'm in."

Caleb knew exactly the word Aaron wouldn't say. *Date.*

They finished the rest of their meal in companionable silence, occasionally stealing glances at one another. Caleb felt like he was back in high school, covertly looking at the boys he found attractive so he wouldn't be caught. Though in this case, he wasn't scared about being discovered. He just didn't want Aaron to think he was pushing too hard to take their friendship out of the friend zone and into romantic territory.

TEN

Last night had been tremendous.

After dinner, Aaron and Caleb sat on the back deck, under the heaters, and talked about what their classmates from high school were up to. Now Caleb was getting ready to walk into Aaron's classroom, and it felt like it was his first day of school. Caleb hadn't expected to be so freaked out when he arrived at the elementary school just after one o'clock.

Through the small window in the door, he saw Aaron at the whiteboard, writing as he talked. He waited for Aaron to hit a stopping point before he knocked. When he finally announced his presence, Aaron continued to talk as he came toward the door, though Caleb couldn't hear a word.

"Welcome," Aaron said as he opened the door. "Class, say hello to our guest, Mr. Carter. He'll be watching this afternoon."

The class of twenty-two became fidgety and chatty, albeit quietly.

"And if you behave, he might answer some questions later and maybe even help us with the lesson."

Aaron raised an eyebrow at Caleb. They'd talked last night about what the lesson would be. But Caleb suddenly felt underprepared and a little bit terrified. Before he left, Aaron had promised he wouldn't embarrass him. Caleb believed that, but his jitters wouldn't calm down.

"Hi, everyone." Caleb raised his hand to wave. The class responded all at once with a cacophony of excited responses.

"We don't really have a good desk for you, so I was thinking you could sit on the bookshelf in the back." Aaron pointed to the low bookshelf under a bulletin board decorated for springtime with a theme of growth.

"Sounds good. Like Mr. Price said, pay attention and do what he says, and I'll answer some questions later."

Caleb went down one of the side aisles, and one of the boys put up a fist, which Caleb bumped as he walked by. The boy grinned, and Caleb winked at him. In the back of the room, he slipped off his jacket, laid it on the bookshelf, and took a seat.

Aaron wasted no time getting back to his lesson, which seemed to center on basics of the US government. Caleb's mind went to *Schoolhouse Rock!* and the "How a Bill Becomes a Law" segment. His teacher showed those clips as part of the lesson. Remembering that made Caleb feel old. Did these kids today even know what that show was?

Aaron's sleeves were rolled up about halfway to his elbows. Caleb noted again how well Aaron dressed for class —black slacks and a blue button-down accented with white pinstripes. The tie, which wasn't loose like it'd been at dinner, was a dark blue. Caleb chastised himself. After seeing what Aaron wore for class, he should've worn slacks rather than just jeans and a sweater. Silently, he took a deep breath to get his nerves under control.

The civics lesson continued for a half hour, and Caleb was just as interested in how Aaron taught and connected with the students. They had a pretty good grip on the topic and even asked some good questions about the election that was coming up in a few months. Since that was a local and state election, Aaron moved seamlessly into talking about how New York operated. He only occasionally referred to the textbook as he talked and drew diagrams.

"So, we need to bring this topic to a close for today. Make sure you do the workbook pages tonight." He pointed to the board and the page numbers. "I'll collect those first thing tomorrow. We'll take a restroom break for five minutes, and then it'll be time for math books."

Aaron went to the door and opened it. He stood in the doorway as most of the kids got up and went into the hall. Caleb smiled at Aaron and mouthed the words "good job" when he looked in his direction. Aaron returned the smile and mouthed "thanks."

Caleb stood and looked at the bulletin board behind him, seeing the pictures the kids had drawn of gardens and flowers, rain and sun, and other spring scenes. A couple of students came up to him while Aaron monitored the hallway.

"What's it like to play for the Rangers?" a student in a Flash T-shirt asked.

"Best thing ever." Caleb sat back on the bookcase so he'd be more at their height.

"I want to play for Philly when I grow up."

"Work hard on your skills, and I bet you can." Caleb loved how the young man's face lit up when he said that.

"Did you play hockey when you went here?"

"I did and I never stopped. It takes a lot of time to get good enough for New York, Philly, or any other team."

"Did you get in trouble for getting hurt?"

"Not at all." Caleb chuckled softly. "The team just wants me to get better and come back."

Another student asked a question. "Did the other guy get in trouble?"

"No, it was an accident. He even apologized after the game. Despite how it may look and how intense the competition is, we really don't want anyone to get hurt."

"Okay, everyone, back in your seats, please."

"Thanks, Mr. Carter," the students said over each other. Fist bumps were traded, and they got back to their desks.

"So, here's something I bet you guys don't know. Mr. Carter was one of the first people I ever taught, back when I was seventeen."

Caleb cringed as Aaron brought up the tutoring. It wasn't Caleb's favorite topic, but it had been necessary at the time.

"He was having a hard time with geometry, and I offered to help him so he could stay on the high school hockey team."

Caleb piped up from the back. "You could say he's partially responsible for getting me into the pros." He played along since he was sure Aaron was going to make this a teachable moment.

"You see, geometry is something that Mr. Carter still uses every day."

A girl in the front row raised her hand and waited for Aaron to call on her before speaking. "Really? I've heard my mom and dad say they never use what they learned in school, especially if they're trying to help my older sister with her homework."

"I used geometry even before I knew what it was, and

the fact that I know it as well as I do makes me a better hockey player."

The class turned to hear Caleb speak.

"Most geometry is all about angles, and angles are crucial to the game. How many of you watch or play regularly?"

Six hands shot up.

"Okay. How many of you have heard of a goalie coming out of his net to decrease the angle?"

Only two hands now.

"Do you know why?" Aaron was already drawing what Caleb described on the white board.

No hands this time.

"It's because moving out in that way makes the net appear smaller to the player, thus reducing the chances of getting a shot by the goalie while also giving them more room to block the shot."

Caleb got a tingly feeling at how well Aaron diagrammed and described the scenario. Aaron added additional lines to the board and drew out even more lines to show various angle scenarios that went beyond what Caleb had considered. The Rangers' goalies would've been impressed.

"Of course, as a forward comes in for a shot, you have to try to force the goalie to reposition." Aaron wrapped up his description, seemingly leaving the kids stunned.

"Now where are the players?" Caleb asked.

Four hands went up.

"How often do you use geometry in a game?"

He got four shrugs in response.

"You use it all the time." Caleb walked to the front of the classroom to draw on the board, but he changed his mind before he picked up the marker. He looked to Aaron. "Can we go outside?"

Aaron looked surprised, and Caleb hoped he hadn't put him in a bad position. "What'd you have in mind?"

Caleb stepped close and whispered in Aaron's ear—the one angled to the whiteboard to help ensure the class couldn't hear. "Show them a couple things using balls—bounce them off the building to help explain angles."

"We can do that," Aaron said quietly back. He turned toward his students. "Want to go outside for a few minutes?"

The class burst into excitement.

"Get your jackets and line up."

As they went out through the gym, Aaron grabbed a couple of baseball-sized rubber balls. On the playground, Aaron brought everyone near a part of the building where there were no windows. Caleb took one of the balls from Aaron and bounced it off the wall a couple times. It would do just fine.

"Mr. Price, could you stand about fifteen feet away, directly across from me?"

Aaron nodded and jogged to his position.

"So, what's the best way for me to send this ball to him?"

Several hands went up, and Caleb picked one.

"Just throw it to him."

"Sure. Straight line, because the shortest distance between two points is a straight line." Caleb threw the ball and Aaron caught it. "So, let's say there were six of you between me and him." Caleb selected six students. "Get in the way."

They went to stand between Caleb and Aaron.

"Now what?"

One of the students between them raised his hand, and Caleb nodded.

"You could just throw it over us."

"True." Caleb nodded at Aaron, who sent the ball back over the students, who all tried to get it out of the air. "That works too. That used an arc to get it over your heads and still get it to me. An arc is just another kind of angle. Now, what would happen if we couldn't throw it over you? In hockey, the puck stays relatively low."

"It doesn't always," said one of the students who had identified as a player after Caleb selected him from the hands that were raised.

"Right. But let's pretend for this moment that it has to stay on the ice. That would make the arc impossible. What are the other options?"

The same student raised his hand again, although slowly, as if he hoped he wouldn't be the only one. Caleb suspected the boy knew the answer and didn't want to spoil the rest of the class, so he had the young man come over to him.

Caleb kneeled down next to the boy. "What's your name?" he asked quietly.

"Byron," he said, nervousness evident in his voice.

"Okay, Byron, whisper the answer to me."

Byron cupped his hand over Caleb's hear and spoke softly. "You're gonna use that wall, like you'd use the boards in a game."

Caleb nodded and smiled at him.

Byron continued to talk quietly but didn't do so directly into Caleb's ear. "My coach always says the boards are your friends because you can use them to redirect the puck."

"Your coach is a smart man. Stay here with me, okay?"

Byron nodded. Caleb stood to address the class. "Okay,

the rest of you figure out where you want to be to stop the ball from reaching Mr. Price."

As suspected, no one got near the wall. They simply piled in the middle between Aaron and Caleb. He saw Aaron squat, almost like a baseball catcher, and that let him know Aaron knew what was going to happen.

"Here it comes."

Caleb considered for a moment. He didn't want to telegraph his intention too much. And the last thing he wanted to do was to hit one of the kids.

He threw the ball at the target he'd picked out. It bounced just as he intended and went to Aaron, who caught it. Caleb high-fived Byron.

The students practiced a few times, throwing against the wall and seeing how hitting different spots would change where the ball would go. Then they talked about how the same ideas could be used to intercept the ball before it got to its target. They played with the geometry for about twenty minutes, then returned to the classroom.

Once they were back inside, Caleb took his spot in the back of the room, and Aaron moved on to a brief science lesson to get the students ready for an upcoming assignment looking at constellations. The class wrapped up with some questions for Caleb, and he answered a few until the bell rang.

When it was just the two of them again, Aaron sat on the edge of his desk next to Caleb. "You're really good with them."

"Not as good as you. Even when the kids don't catch on quickly, you're so patient."

"You really clicked with Byron today, and that was awesome. He's smart but doesn't like participating, so the fact you let him stand out as the person who knew the wall was the answer is outstanding. I don't think he'll forget that, and hopefully, it'll pull him out of his shell more."

Caleb was proud and grinned broadly. "I couldn't have imagined when you were helping me get this stuff right all those years ago that I'd actually help you teach it."

"You remember it and use it. Means I didn't waste my time."

"Good teachers can make things stick."

They held each other's gazes for a moment and only broke it when there was a knock at the door and Pam entered.

"How are two of my favorite people? Is it true you let my brother teach?"

Aaron and Caleb briefly recounted their afternoon for her before they had to leave for hockey practice.

ELEVEN

Aaron wrapped up the after-school club he had with kids who were into science. He'd run a similar club in LA and was thrilled when it was approved as part of this job. The club did simple experiments and broke things down to the level that third-through-fifth graders could comprehend. He enjoyed working with the club and hoped he'd end up inspiring a scientist or two in the long run. Today had been a particularly good day because a couple of students brought in things to share—experiments of their own construction based on what they'd learned.

"Glad to see you didn't blow anything up today." Pam stood in the classroom doorway as he finished putting away the equipment he kept for the club. "I was worried when Jennifer Baldwin came in with all those electronics this morning."

Aaron laughed at Pam's stern face. "You never were one for science. How was your day? I heard there were issues at lunch."

Pam rolled her eyes, entered, and set her bag and jacket on a desk. "I felt like I was living a real-life version of *Mean*

Girls. I've never heard such things from kids this age before. I suspended two fourth graders and put three others in detention. It was ridiculous. Tomorrow I get to meet with the parents. I'm sure that's going to be awesome." She seemed annoyed just thinking about it.

"Want to go unwind with some coffee?"

"I'd love that." She said, sounding as if he'd just made the best suggestion ever. "I've missed that this week, with you on hockey duty. How'd that happen, anyway? I know you like hockey, but to help out?"

Aaron gathered his things as Pam talked. "I got recruited at the same time Caleb did."

"Did he force you into that?"

"No," he answered quickly, because Pam seemed ready to pounce on Caleb. "I offered all on my own, thank you."

"Okay. Sorry." Pam eyed him suspiciously. "It's just not like you. I know you like your afternoon time to decompress and get things set for the next day."

"This is kinda fun, though."

"I should come watch. See you two out there together."

Aaron didn't know what to say. If Pam saw them together, would she notice anything but friendship between them? Aaron's guard was down more and more as he lost the battle against Caleb's gentle kindness, like how he'd worked with Bryon during the geometry lesson. On the ice, since Aaron spent time standing around and directing traffic, he'd end up watching Caleb if nothing was happening around him. More than once, Caleb had caught him and sent a smile his direction. Aaron had to stop doing that. Caleb didn't need to feel led on.

"I'll meet you at the café," Pam said as they walked out and Aaron locked the door.

He was more confused than ever about Caleb.

Coaching—and teaching—with him was far better than he'd imagined. Granted, he wasn't exactly coaching with Caleb, but they were a part of the same activity. Teaching together had left Aaron exhilarated. They'd been in perfect sync, and Caleb's idea to go outside for a real-world demonstration had been inspired.

How would Pam feel if he and Caleb became a thing? She'd been his sounding board for years during high school and college, and he wanted advice. But he didn't want to upset her, and most definitely couldn't have her talking to Caleb about it. She'd always been good with keeping his secrets, so that was less of a concern than her being pissed that he wanted to go out with her little brother. He'd seen her protective side when she'd griped about Caleb's choices —and she'd been pretty harsh about some of Aaron's too.

She'd be more upset later if Aaron kept it from her and something did come from it. Aaron shook as head—where had that come from? Nothing could come of it. Sometimes his brain didn't know what it was talking about.

They drove to the café, got their coffee, and settled into their favorite table, alongside the big window that looked out on Main Street.

"We got the final tally from the school carnival," Pam said proudly. "It was the most successful fundraiser in school history."

"That's fantastic," Aaron said. He knew that Caleb's celebrity would help their local event but couldn't have imagined how big of a draw he'd actually be.

"Even better," she said, leaning in conspiratorially, "today the school received a huge check from a certain hockey player who we both happen to know. He matched every dollar we raised!"

Of course he did.

Caleb was generous and kind. Talented and irresistibly attractive.

Like a sexy knight in shining hockey gear, he'd ridden into town, all perfect and noble, seeming determined to wear down Aaron's resolve. Aaron was no swooning damsel in distress, though if he were honest with himself, being swept up in Caleb's muscular embrace held a certain appeal.

"You don't look pleased." Pam held her coffee cup in two hands and looked over the top of it at Aaron. "What's going on?"

"What're you talking about?" There was no way she hadn't heard the defensiveness in his tone. Was there?

Pam gave him the look she gave to students who were sent to her office for doing something wrong. The one that said she could wait it out until he spilled the beans.

"That won't work on me." He looked at her, willing himself to not succumb.

After a minute or so of the staring contest, she relented. "No fair. You've been around me too much."

"Ha!"

"Seriously, though. What's up?"

"Please don't get mad, but I really need someone to talk to."

"Oh my God. Are you in trouble? Did someone die?"

"No. No." He shook his head as he laughed nervously. He took a deep breath before blurting out, "I think I might like your brother."

There. He'd said it. He'd gotten it out.

"Of course you do," Pam said with a dismissive wave of her hand. "You've known him forever. You've been—" She stopped cold. She was never at a loss for words, so Aaron expected the worst. "Oh, wait. You *like* like him. That's fantastic!" A huge smile spread across her face.

Aaron examined his coffee, trying to hide from anyone who might be looking their direction since Pam was rather loud in her proclamation.

She put her hand over her mouth as she realized it too. "Sorry," she said, restraining her voice. "Why on earth would you be worried telling me that?"

"I've seen some of the reactions you've had to his boyfriends."

"Totally different. This is you."

Again, his heart betrayed him. He shouldn't have said anything, and yet he couldn't keep his mouth shut. "Can I tell you something else, then, as my friend and maybe not as his sister?"

"Um. Okay." She sounded as dubious as Aaron felt.

"First, we're not dating or anything, but I think I want to even though I'm not sure if...." There were some things he wasn't comfortable telling Pam. "I can't tell if he wants a real date. He might be flirting, or maybe I just want to believe he is. I don't know if it's right to even ask him. I live here. He's in New York. He's a major hockey star, and I'm just a schoolteacher who can barely stand up on skates sometimes. There's no reason to think it could last. But—"

"He makes your heart do somersaults in your chest," Pam interrupted.

"Exactly." He couldn't lie about that.

"Let me tell you about my brother. You know the guys he's dated over the past few years? The ones I've mocked as not being right for him? You know, sometimes those are a setup, right?"

Aaron nodded. "Yeah. He told me that over dinner."

"Oh, okay. He usually keeps that under pretty tight wraps."

"He also said he wasn't doing that anymore."

Pam's eyes widened. "Good for him. Anyway, even guys he's actually dating haven't made him happy. They either don't know what it means to date someone who travels like he does, or they expect it to be a lot more glamorous than it is. I honestly don't even know the last time he was on a date."

Aaron wondered if maybe dinner had been more of a date than either of them had realized. "I don't know how I'd do in a relationship with someone who lived somewhere else. Travel's one thing, but he doesn't even live here."

"Have you two talked about that?"

"No. Oh God!" This time it was Aaron who was too loud. "It's hard enough talking to you. I think we're both dodging that discussion. He seems less hesitant that I am, but... I don't know." He cast his gaze down to his coffee mug.

"You two need to talk. He's only got a week left here. Don't let that get away. I think you'd make a great couple. He's more like you than you might think. He's not the big-shot athlete with an ego to match. He's just Caleb, and I've never seen him behave any other way."

"Thanks," Aaron said. "Just between us, right?"

"Best friend's honor." Pam held up her hand to swear. "If he asks me anything, though, I won't hesitate to tell him to go for it. Just like I'm telling you."

Aaron nodded before moving them on to safer topics, like what had gone down on that week's episode of *The Voice*.

TWELVE

Watching Caleb, who was dressed in sweatpants and a sleeveless T-shirt, his face glistening with sweat and the edges of his blond hair damp, captivated Aaron. All he could think about was how Caleb might look after a round or two of hot sex. He banished those dangerous thoughts as quickly as possible.

"My God, that feels good." Caleb's face showed pure happiness as he glided to a stop next to Aaron.

"You make that look so easy. Like you've never been away from it."

"I usually hate rehab skating, but I'm kind of enjoying it. There's some soreness that I have to work out afterward, but it's nothing I haven't been through before. What's going to be fun is skating with the kids."

"They're going to love that, but make sure you stop if you need to."

Caleb nodded. "I don't think I've got to worry about overdoing it with them. And you're looking confident. How's it feel?"

"Better. Less wobbly."

They'd worked with Ian for about fifteen minutes before the previous practice. The refresher on skating basics was exactly what Aaron had needed. At least he wouldn't be a burden while he was trying to help.

Caleb put his hand out as if he wanted to dance. "Skate with me."

It was an invitation, but it also wasn't a question.

"Okay." Aaron pushed his nerves away and put his hand in Caleb's. Despite the chill of the rink, Caleb's hand was warm and enveloped Aaron's. He'd avoided touching like this so often over the past few days that, with the pent-up anticipation, Aaron vibrated with excitement that he hoped he could keep from Caleb. He hadn't felt like this in a long while. Maybe it was time to allow it.

"Here we go. Slow and easy around the rink to warm up."

Aaron nodded. There weren't words for the mix of emotions he felt. He was scared he'd stumble and wipe them both out. There was also the incredible energy pouring from Caleb. It threatened to make him giddy.

Aaron maintained his composure and managed to remain upright. When Caleb gently sped up, he followed suit.

"You're doing great," Caleb said on the third lap.

"I think the lesson on the proper stance to maintain my center of gravity is what did it."

Caleb's extra squeeze on Aaron's hand sent shockwaves through him. This could've been a date, a real romantic date —that is, if they weren't about to be besieged by a couple dozen kids.

"Let's try something different." Caleb released Aaron, and it was like a lifeline had been lost. Aaron resisted the urge to reach out as Caleb skated a few paces ahead and spun around to face him.

"Show-off." Aaron smirked but didn't lose his speed or balance.

"All part of the training package." Caleb smirked right back. "Now, do your best to keep up."

Caleb sped up, and Aaron cautiously did the same. It was difficult not to focus solely on Caleb effortlessly gliding backward, even as they moved around the curved areas of the rink. It took less than a full lap, though, for Aaron to maintain a fairly equal distance from Caleb. They did so for a couple of laps as Caleb varied his speed, requiring Aaron to constantly make adjustments.

"Ready for the advanced class?"

"Bring it." Aaron's nervousness stayed away. Instead, he smiled with pride as Caleb simply nodded with a twinkle in his eye Aaron liked a lot.

"We're going to move away from the boards and go more zigzaggy." Caleb didn't wait for a response. He led Aaron across the ice in seemingly random patterns. It wasn't too fast and Caleb was a lot smoother in the diagonal moves, but Aaron did okay. "Looking good. Let's speed it up."

Caleb was suddenly a number of strides away from Aaron, and he tried to use the skills he'd learned to seamlessly add the needed velocity. He sputtered at first, but soon had closed the gap between them. This game went on for several minutes until Caleb declared they would stop in the corner.

Caleb came to a smooth stop, but Aaron had issues with the hockey stop they'd practiced last time.

"Just do the snowplow," Caleb called out as he saw what was happening, but it was too late. As Aaron struggled to stop, he saw Caleb brace for impact. Caleb caught him in an embrace as Aaron's remaining momentum pushed them into the boards. "I've got you."

Aaron planted his feet firmly under himself as he stood face to face with Caleb. "Thanks." He sounded out of breath, partially because of the terror of being out of control, but also because Caleb held him and they were close enough to kiss. Aaron relished looking into Caleb's deep blue eyes. He was gorgeous and being this close made that abundantly clear. "Um. I'm. Well. Sorry." Aaron was mortified and would be happy if he could simply melt into the ice.

Caleb offered a shy smile but didn't avert his eyes. "It's okay. I've had far worse hits."

Despite the fact he liked it there, Aaron pushed back just enough that Caleb dropped his hold. "I'd never hear the end of it if you got hurt again trying to teach me to skate."

"As long as you'd play doctor, it'd be okay."

Aaron's face heated, and he had no doubt he was a fiery red. Was Caleb playing with him? Or—

"Guys, look!" There was excited chatter as the team came onto the ice. "Coach Carter's on skates!"

"I didn't realize it was time. I should get things set up." Aaron made an awkward turn away and saw Ian and the other volunteers coming onto the ice behind the players. He looked back at Caleb. Aaron hesitated, and Caleb stayed focused on him. Aaron wished he could steal a quick kiss before he joined the others. "Thanks for the skate."

"Anytime."

He gave a quick nod before he took off to get the cones for warmups. He felt a lot more confident despite the almost fall. While he worked, he kept an eye on Caleb, who hadn't seemed flustered by their close proximity. Caleb toweled the sweat off his head at the bench and put on his Rangers hoodie. Then he took off skating with the team, and they stayed near him as if he were the Pied Piper. As they went by Aaron, he could hear the constant chatter the team kept up with Caleb.

After a few minutes, Rick came out on the ice and whistled the group together to start their drills through the cones. The players scrambled to the four corners. Aaron was already stationed at one of the corners.

Caleb surprised Aaron when he lined up with other players. "Mind if I go first?"

The kids nodded, and Aaron certainly said nothing. As far as he was concerned, Caleb could do whatever he wanted.

Caleb bolted as soon as the whistle blew. He did the forward, backward, and figure eights that were required. He was fast, at least by Aaron's measure. Caleb looked happy and ready to go again. This glimpse of speedy Caleb in his element excited Aaron. It was only a sprint down the ice, but it captivated Aaron more than seeing him play on TV ever had.

When Caleb arrived back at Aaron's corner, Aaron offered a subtle thumbs-up. What he wanted to do was hug him, this time on purpose instead of falling into him. Yes, he wanted Caleb. The more time they spent together, the more Aaron was happier than he'd been in—well, longer than he could remember. Moving back to Foster Grove had turned one corner of his life, and he was starting to remember what happiness felt like. There were so many challenges involved in dating Caleb, but it might be worth the risk to leave his LA baggage in the past.

So much to think about.

Rick blew the whistle. "Let's go, Carter. You're holding up the line."

The whistle snapped Aaron out of his thoughts. Why was Rick yelling at Caleb? More importantly, why was Caleb looking Aaron's direction when it happened?

"Sorry," Caleb called out before he took off.

What had distracted Caleb? Was he thinking the same thing Aaron was?

The flutter of Aaron's heart drove home the point of what he wanted. He just had to figure out if it was right to want it.

THIRTEEN

CALEB SAT in the last row of the bleachers. He liked sitting up high during games so he could see more of the ice and watch the plays develop. This was the first time he'd seen the kids in a game, and he planned to take notes so he'd have things to discuss on Monday.

As he watched the team warm up, he worked to push away his sadness at missing yet another game with New York. He'd been out a couple dozen games, and while he was just a few days from going back, he was annoyed every time they were on the ice and he wasn't. At least yesterday afternoon's check-in with the local physical therapist and the Skype call with the team doc had gone well.

"Hey."

Aaron's voice startled him. He hadn't known Aaron would be coming to the game. They'd made no weekend plans—Caleb couldn't decide how to move forward since there were still mixed signals between them, and Aaron hadn't discussed anything after Friday's practice either.

"What a nice surprise. Have a seat." Caleb patted the empty space next to him.

Aaron sat, keeping his cup of hot chocolate in his gloved hands. "I wanted to see what these guys look like in a game since those start-and-stop scrimmages don't really give much of a clue."

"I decided it'd be useful to give them some notes from a game, so here I am." Caleb inhaled to take in more of the chocolate aroma coming from Aaron's travel mug. Even with the lid on, the scent was strong. "Where'd you get the cocoa?"

"Picked it up at FG on the way over."

"Figures," Caleb said, sadly. "I should've thought of that. I got a cup of coffee here, and it wasn't good." He pointed to the cup next to him, which was hardly touched.

Aaron held out the mug toward Caleb. "Have some."

"You sure?"

"As long as you don't have cooties." Aaron made the gesture again, and this time Caleb took it.

"I was inoculated a couple months ago. I can show you the proof if you want." Caleb reached around to his back pocket for his wallet.

Aaron's soft laugh threatened to make Caleb's insides burst because it was so endearing. "That's okay. I trust you."

Caleb bumped his shoulder into Aaron and laughed along with him. The cocoa sharing, the good-natured ribbing, the bump—it all felt like something a couple would do. The more these little things happened, the more he wanted to know what coupledom would be like with Aaron.

Caleb took a sip and had to restrain himself from drinking too much. "That is *so* good." He handed the mug back. "Nate should open a café here."

"Nate ran a café annex out at Grove Park when the outdoor rink was up this past winter."

"That sounds perfect. Skating, drinking cocoa. Please tell me you went."

"You've seen my skating skills, which kinda sucked until recently," Aaron said sheepishly. "Skating while drinking a hot beverage would not have ended well."

"This winter I'm coming to take you out for a skate, then." Caleb looked at Aaron, who held the mug halfway to his lips. "If you'd be into it."

"I'd like that," Aaron said softly before drinking.

The horn sounded over the big scoreboard, indicating the game was about to start. Both men turned their attention to the ice as the teams lined up for the face-off. After some grappling, the other side won the puck and the game was underway.

Caleb occasionally made notes on his phone while they talked about what was happening on the ice. Caleb, however, was sometimes distracted by Aaron's quiet acceptance of a skating date, which he couldn't stop thinking about. He was also being incredibly sweet by sharing the cocoa, which they passed back and forth routinely during the first period until it was gone.

It was like they'd relaxed to the point they'd fallen momentarily into a future where they were together. Caleb liked it. He hadn't been this comfortable around a man he was attracted to in longer than he cared to admit.

"They play well," Aaron said as the final buzzer sounded. Their team won three to one. As the game ended and the opponents shook hands, the spectators left the bleachers and either headed into the lobby or gathered rinkside to talk to the players. Caleb and Aaron continued to sit as the others left.

"Rick's done a good job with them. They learn quick. I

want to work with them on face-offs. I think I can give them some pointers on how to anticipate better."

"I definitely see coaching in your future between seeing you work with the kids here and the way you taught a little geometry the other day."

"It's a definite possibility for retirement. I always enjoy it." Caleb stood. "You ready to get out of the cold?" He hadn't missed that Aaron sometimes shivered despite the gloves, hat, and heavier jacket.

"Yeah. Sorry, was it that obvious?"

"Little bit." Caleb smiled, and the smile he got back warmed him more than a coat ever could.

"It's a lot different when you're not moving around, like at practices."

"That's why you wear layers." Caleb moved the neckline of his sweatshirt to show the two layers beneath it.

"I'll know better next time," Aaron said as they descended the bleachers. "What are you up to the rest of the afternoon?"

"I hadn't planned that far ahead. What about you?"

"I'm headed over to the park. There's a craft fair today, and some of the students are manning the bake sale booth to fund a field trip to Albany. I want to swing by and lend some support. Wanna come?"

"Sure," Caleb said, thrilled to be asked. They moved quickly through the lobby. Caleb didn't want to get caught up with any of the players who might delay them. He'd see the team on Monday.

"So, I'll meet you there," Caleb said when they got to his SUV.

"See you in five." Aaron waved and continued on to his car.

Caleb was ecstatic with the turn the afternoon had

taken. Not only had he unexpectedly spent the game with Aaron, but now they were doing more.

Caleb ended up at the park first. Once he was out of his car, he looked across the green grass. With the sunny, warmer afternoon, kids were out on the playground in force, while a group of teens played ultimate Frisbee nearby. The craft fair was set up around the fountain. The fair was considerably bigger than he remembered it being the few times his parents had dragged him here. The playground was different too, with a climbing wall as its centerpiece.

Aaron pulled his car next to the SUV, and Caleb turned to greet him.

"You looked deep in thought," Aaron said to him over the roofs of the cars.

"This was probably my second-favorite place to hang out as a kid."

"I'm pretty sure I know what the first was."

Aaron was more at ease than Caleb had seen him so far on the trip. He hoped it would continue, since his time home was coming to an end in a few days. Maybe asking him on an actual date wouldn't be the worst thing.

"I'd always train through here too." Caleb stayed with the safe topic of the park for now. "It was my favorite place to run lap after lap in the off-season since I didn't play any other sports." His gaze shifted to Aaron. "Did you come out here much?"

"You know, I never really did." He shrugged. "I know the town does movies here in the summer, and I'll probably come out for some of those. As a kid, though, I wasn't very outdoorsy."

"True." Caleb nodded. "You were usually stuck in a book, as I remember."

"Sounds about right."

"Can I tell you something I've never told anyone else?" Caleb steered them away from the craft fair and into some trees. He brought them to a stop at a water fountain next to a running path.

"Of course."

"When I was a freshman, I was running out here one morning before school and ended up alongside Ralph Tyler. He was a junior on the track team. Remember him at all?"

"Not so much from school. I know him now because he owns a gym. His daughter is a fifth grader too."

"Oh. Maybe I shouldn't spread gossip, then." Caleb put his hand over his mouth.

"You can't start a story and then not finish it." Aaron pulled at Caleb's hand, which made him clamp it to his face tighter because he liked Aaron pulling on it. Finally, he let him pull it free.

"Okay. It's just as much gossip about me, I guess. We were running and he was really pushing me because he was the true runner, after all. Anyway, we paused right here to get some water, and while I was stretching against that tree, he kissed me and I kinda kissed him back."

Aaron involuntarily gave a nervous laugh. "Wow."

"Right. I thought I was maybe into guys, but I hadn't done anything because I didn't want to get in trouble. It was such a fumble, but energizing at the same time. We heard someone on the path, so we didn't kiss for long, and he swore me to never tell. Which I haven't until now." Caleb chuckled but stopped at Aaron's surprised look. "Sorry. Too much information?"

"No. I was just...." Aaron looked away, leaving Caleb sure he'd said the completely wrong thing. It wasn't like he was coming out to Aaron, but he was left feeling like he'd screwed up instead of simply revealing part of his past. "I was such a confused basket case during high school. Terrified someone would find me out and make life more hell than it already was, being the bookish guy."

"You always seemed happy," Caleb said, facing Aaron.

"I was okay. I didn't have a tortured high school experience. Names were called, occasionally books knocked off desks, or whatever. I made sure to stay in my lane, though, you know?"

Caleb nodded. He'd been lucky he had the jock role to play, which tended to keep him out of any bully's sights.

"When I was a freshman in college and finally taking some chances since I wasn't at home anymore, I was at a frat party and ended up in the basement of the house with a very drunk junior member. I was newly pledged, and he ordered me to follow him, which, of course, I did. I thought we were going to bring up more stuff for the party, but instead he took me in a dark corner and started kissing me."

The way his features suddenly clouded over stabbed at Caleb's heart. He took Aaron's hand and squeezed gently.

"You don't have to finish the story."

"It's really not a bad ending. The kisses weren't great—he tasted like cheap beer. He groped me a little, but we were interrupted because someone else came downstairs. He quickly pulled back and shoved a case of soda in my hands and took one for himself. He made a quick retreat. He either didn't remember it or ignored that it ever happened."

Aaron flexed his hand in Caleb's, and he squeezed gently as they gazed at each other.

Caleb slowly leaned in, giving himself an out if Aaron's expression changed. The sad look disappeared, replaced by a shy smile. Caleb took that for a yes, closed his eyes, and placed a soft kiss on Aaron's lips.

Aaron kissed him back, matching Caleb's gentleness. As their lips stayed together, Caleb interlocked his fingers with Aaron's. Caleb, emboldened by Aaron's reaction, slid his tongue across Aaron's lips, but he didn't force it inside. The last thing he wanted was to go too far or too fast.

Caleb pulled back just enough so he could speak. "I hope you're not going to run away."

Aaron shook his head slowly. "No way. Not after my first kiss from Caleb Carter."

"It's not really our first," Caleb said, smiling shyly and feeling, for a moment, like a teenager again.

Aaron's brows knitted together in confusion. "What are you talking about? Of course it is."

"Remember when I gave you the trophy when you graduated?"

"Of course."

"Well, I hugged you, and my lips brushed against your cheek when you pulled away," Caleb whispered, close to Aaron. "I've always considered that our first kiss."

Aaron raised a hand to his cheek as if that might conjure the memory. "What do you know. I'd had a kiss from you all this time and didn't know it."

"Well, it was subtle, barely a kiss at all, so I'll forgive you for not remembering."

Aaron chuckled softly as they gazed at each other.

"Come on," Caleb said, wanting to break the moment before it had any chance to get weird. "Let's go buy some baked goods to support a good cause."

FOURTEEN

"DIMITRI!" Caleb shouted into the phone as he connected the call. He was just off the ice from his late-morning practice and rehab session, sitting on the bleachers adjacent to the rink.

Dimitri Stanislov and Caleb arrived in New York in the same season and became fast friends. Dimitri was traded from Minnesota, where he'd spent a couple of years after being drafted straight out of a Denver high school, while Caleb went to the Rangers from the University of Maine. Dimitri was a couple years older and was a top wing, even winning the Ross Trophy three years ago as the top scorer in the league. The two bonded over being the first out players for the Rangers and enduring the media spotlight that brought with it in their first season. Luckily, it faded quickly once they proved themselves on the ice.

"I'm surprised to hear from you since you guys are out west. What's goin' on?"

"It's good. You know, usual road stuff. We're about to fly to Vancouver. Not the same without you, man. I miss my roommate."

"That just means you can have overnight guests, and I know you like that."

Dimitri grunted. "Yeah. But it also means I don't get enough sleep because you don't come back to the room to gently show them out. I was good last night, though. Phoenix didn't put any interesting guys in my path."

Dimitri loved road hookups. Caleb played wingman sometimes, and other times he just let him do his thing.

"So, to what do I owe this unexpected call?"

"You're really going to play it that way, huh?" Dimitri was fishing for something, but Caleb had no clue what.

"You know everything going on. I'm still on track to be back next week."

"You're kissing some guy."

Caleb was dumbstruck. Sure, some people in town might have seen, but—

"How do you know about that?" Caleb hadn't known how to talk about what was going on with Aaron, so he hadn't said anything to Dimitri. And the kiss had only happened yesterday. He'd barely had time to process it himself. He looked around the rink and was glad it was early on a Sunday morning. There were few people around, and no one on the rink he occupied.

"It's all over the internet, my friend. You'd know that if you actually paid attention. I'm surprised you haven't heard from Grant. He's gotta be fielding calls and messages."

Caleb had never embraced social media. He had official Twitter and Facebook pages because the team insisted on it. He didn't have personal profiles on any site. He preferred to see people in person or communicate with texts and emails. He understood, however, the need to have his professional life covered, which was one of the main reasons he'd hired Grant.

He looked at the phone screen and saw two missed calls and a text from Grant. He was more than competent, so Caleb was confident everything was under control. He'd call once he finished with Dimitri, though.

"Yeah. Looks like I missed a couple calls while I was skating." He nestled the phone awkwardly against his shoulder so he could unlace his skates.

"Whatever. Let's get to the good stuff. Who's the guy? He looked kinda cute from what I could see. And the kiss in a park is so *you* on the romantic scale."

Caleb sighed. How did he want to put this? He could talk to Dimitri, no problem. But there wasn't an actual label to put on what he and Aaron were doing. Plus, there was the problem that this thing was out there in the world. He'd need to let Aaron, and probably Pam, know too.

"Did I lose you?"

"No," Caleb said quickly. "Just trying to figure out what to say."

"What?" Dimitri was surprised. "That's never been a problem before."

"His name's Aaron. We've known each other for forever. We've reconnected since I've been here."

"I'll say. I thought your first guy was in college."

"He's not my first.... He's never been...." Caleb hated sputtering like this. "He was my tutor, and my sister's best friend. He's helping coach the youth team, and we've hung out a bit and...." Another sigh. "There's something there. I can't figure out how he feels about it, though he did kiss me and we hung out and ended up helping at a bake sale yesterday."

"That's way too adorable."

"Shut up." If they'd been in the same room, Caleb

would've shoved Dimitri for using that singsong voice with him.

"You know I don't do adorable. I'd probably have had his clothes off against that tree and fucked him silly."

Caleb laughed. "I've missed you and that crudeness."

"Glad to be of service." Silence took hold for a moment before Dimitri continued. "You should just let it go. You come back to New York in three days, and you won't have time for him. Take his cute ass to bed so you can say you tried it and then pack up and come home."

Caleb couldn't laugh this time. Dimitri was crude, but he always had Caleb's back. This time, though, he didn't much care for the advice. "I don't know if I can do that."

"What? Come home?"

"No. Let it go."

"He's really cast a spell on you. You've never gone on like this about a guy. Not even that model from a couple years ago."

"No one's made me feel like this. I almost tried to take him home last night, but I can't do that until I know it's something we both want."

"You don't think he wants to fuck a hockey star?"

"Dimitri!"

Finally out of his skates, he was able to get the phone back in his hand. He slipped into his sneakers, which he kept laced so he could do just that.

"Sometimes I forget you're not me. I'm way out of my depth here. Knowing you, though, I think you and your tutor need to get this sorted. Maybe he's like me and will be satisfied with one sexed-up night."

Caleb groaned.

"*Or*, he might be like you and want to settle down after a period of courtship."

Caleb burst out laughing, not believing what he'd just heard. "*Period of courtship?* Really?"

"I know how the world works for you romantic types, even if I don't get it."

"You're right about one thing. We need to talk. And now that the picture's out, it's going to have to be sooner rather than later."

"You really like him, don't you?" Dimitri had rarely sounded so earnest.

"I think so, yeah. He makes me feel settled, relaxed. You know how antsy I can get."

"Well, that tiny town of yours isn't too far from the city. You could get up there a couple times a month during the season."

That was true. Caleb had the means to do almost anything he wanted. He was well paid, and the only thing he'd really splurged on was his loft in Manhattan, and that was only because it was hard not to spend a lot on a place to live in the city. He could drive up as he'd always done or fly to Albany. Plenty of options were available if he and Aaron wanted him to use them.

"Talk to him."

"Who are you?" Caleb appreciated the advice but was puzzled to get this from Dimitri. It sounded more like things Pam would say, and he couldn't talk to her about this. Not with Aaron being her best friend. What was she going to think when she saw the picture? And it would be *when* not *if*. If she didn't find it on her own, someone else would surely show it to her.

"I know how to be your wingman too, even if you rarely make use of those services."

His phone beeped. He glanced at the screen and saw Pam's ID.

"Pam's calling. I should take this. Can you send me a link to the picture so I don't have to search for it?"

"You got it. If you need to talk, I'll be in Vancouver around noon."

"Thanks." He keyed over to Pam's call. "Hey, Pam." He decided to sound like he had no clue what she might be calling about.

"So it seems my little brother has something he needs to tell me."

It seemed the proverbial cat was already out of the bag. Just his luck. "You've seen it?"

"It's hard to miss. A lot of people are wondering who Caleb Carter is kissing."

"Shit. Does Aaron know yet?"

"I don't know. Haven't heard from him today."

"You're not mad?"

"Of course not. Maybe disappointed you didn't tell me something might be going on. I want you both happy. Can this end up in a way neither of you gets hurt?"

"I hope so." Caleb's voice was strained in a way that confused him as he heard it.

"Oh, little brother, you've fallen hard. No wonder the picture looks like something out of a movie. Whoever took it knew how to take a good shot."

Caleb's phone chirped. "Hang on a second. I just got the photo. I'm going to have a look." He clicked on the text message and then the link. The picture was full screen on one of the Rangers fan sites. His chest tightened as a wave of emotion flooded over him. Despite the invasion of privacy, Caleb had to admit that the picture was... perfect. They stood in profile, their lips gently pressed together. A fleeting intimate moment captured by cell phone. They looked happy—as if they'd been together for years rather than days. "Wow." The word was choked out, and he cleared his throat. "That's...."

"Exactly," Pam said softly. "Please figure out what you guys want and go for it. Or at least decide together to walk away from it."

The phone's call waiting chimed again. This time the display showed Grant.

"I'll try not to hurt him. I promise."

"I know. Try not to hurt yourself either. I love you both. Whatever happens won't change that."

"Thanks. I should go. Grant's calling."

"Uh-oh. I bet he's not happy. Call me later if you need to talk."

"Okay." He clicked over to Grant. "Hey, Grant. Sorry."

"No need to be sorry. I just wish you'd told me you were seeing someone. It's one thing to manage responses to the pictures and posts of you coaching kids, but a heads-up you're on a date would've been good just so I'd know what to say. Isn't that guy the teacher from the carnival? The one we walked out with?"

As they talked, Caleb packed his duffel bag so he could leave as soon as he was done with the calls. "It is. How bad is it out there?"

"I wouldn't say bad. Except for Phil, who thinks this is the worst thing ever. People are mostly curious who the guy is. Some are questioning why you're dating when you should be rehabbing. There's some homophobes saying stupid stuff, but I'm just deleting that crap."

"Phil called about this? Why?"

"You know him," Grant said wearily. "Always worried about your new contract and how something like this might affect the negotiations. He wants you to call as soon as possible."

"Anything else?"

"You should think about making a statement, for the fans. Explain that it's not something random. They're used to that sort of tabloid behavior from Dimitri, but not you. That's just my guidance. It's up to you. I can craft a message, or you can, or we can work on it together. You're a private guy, so there's no reason to go overboard."

"I'll get you a response that you can post after I talk to Aaron. I'll call Phil back too, although not right away."

"Okay. I'm here if you need anything, and I'll let you know if something major comes up. I doubt it will, though. So far people are pretty happy for you."

"Thanks, Grant." As he was disconnected the call, he left the rink because he needed to see Aaron.

FIFTEEN

AARON SPENT Sunday morning as he often did—relaxing on the couch, enjoying coffee, and catching up on TV he'd missed from the previous week. By noon, he'd laughed and cried and was ready to get on with the rest of his day.

What he hadn't expected, when taking his phone off the charger, was a flood of text messages, emails, and Facebook notifications from the past few hours. There was nothing that could possibly warrant so much chatter. It took only one of the notifications, however, to see that he was, in fact, the news.

"How the hell did that happen?" he asked the empty apartment.

No good could come from this. Caleb would surely distance himself as soon as he saw it. It would be a distraction from returning to the team. He'd come up here, after all, to rehab, not to get into a compromising situation with a local.

Aaron scrolled through the messages. The comments ranged from congratulatory to downright mean-spirited. Aaron had read less than a fourth of them before he tossed the phone on the table. How'd they even identify him? His face was mostly obscured.

A knock at the door startled him. He was in sweats and a T-shirt, with bed head, and now someone was at the door. He couldn't face anyone like this.

Another knock.

"It's Caleb." His deep voice reverberated through the door, making Aaron want to hide. "Please, Aaron."

He couldn't resist the pleading in the voice. Maybe Caleb wasn't mad. Maybe he hadn't seen it. Although that was unlikely, since Grant would've have alerted him, if nothing else. But why would he just show up here?

Aaron caught his reflection in the mirror by the door as he shuffled past. He looked a horror. "Hey." He sounded as upbeat as he could while opening the door.

"Oh, did I wake you?" Caleb looked apologetic, holding a bag from FG Café.

"No, no. I'm just lazy on Sundays." Aaron looked behind Caleb, out at the street. He saw nothing unusual out there. "Come on in."

"You thought it was the press or something, didn't you?" he asked, stepping inside and closing the door. "You've seen the picture."

Aaron nodded. "I'm so sorry. I can't imagine—"

Caleb held up his hand, interrupting Aaron. "Stop. It's certainly not your fault someone decided to snap a picture or that it was posted and shared all over the internet." He shrugged. "Whatever. I'm certainly not sorry we kissed."

"Really?" Did Caleb mean that? How could he?

"Really. I brought some lunch over so we could talk." He held up the bag. "Nate gave me something to go."

"You've got pull," Aaron said, trying not to think too

much about the situation. "Word is he doesn't usually do to-go from the restaurant."

"I told him it was important, and I think he knew why. Is this going to cause problems for you? The photo, I mean?" he asked, making his way to the small kitchen. Caleb pulled the containers from the bag and set the food out on the counter while Aaron got plates from the cabinet and utensils from the silverware drawer.

"For me? I don't think so. I'm an out, gay, single school-teacher. They might not expect me to be kissing a star athlete in the park, but I don't think it'll be an issue. What about you? I doubt a hookup is what your team was expecting while you were out of town healing from an injury."

Caleb stopped opening containers and fixed his gaze on Aaron. "What we did was hardly a hookup. *You're* not a hookup. Far from it."

Before Aaron could react, Caleb's lips met Aaron's, and he surrendered to the kiss. Caleb's tongue parted Aaron's lips, and Aaron couldn't hold back a moan as Caleb embraced him tightly. Aaron's eyes closed as he relished the kiss.

There was nothing he could do but hang on for the ride. Aaron's tongue met Caleb's in a fight for positioning. This wasn't the soft kiss they'd shared yesterday. While that had given Aaron goose bumps and a slight hard-on, this electri-fied him from head to toe and caused his cock to ache even in the loose confines of his sweats. That hadn't happened in a long time, and every fiber of him was very aware of the need this awakened.

Their moaning got more intense as they kissed deeper. The scruff on Caleb's face was exactly what Aaron liked to feel scraping against his own. He took opportunities to nibble on his upper lip to feel more of it. He pulled away from Caleb's mouth just enough to run a line of kisses around his jawline so he could nibble and nuzzle the dark blond whiskers. Caleb shuddered, and Aaron kept it up until he had to return to Caleb's mouth.

Caleb suddenly stopped with his lips gently pushed against Aaron's. Aaron opened his eyes in confusion and found Caleb looking at him.

"I want to figure this out with you," Caleb said, keeping him wrapped in his embrace. "To talk about ways it *can* work. I want to date you—to see what that's like—and get to know everything about you."

Aaron shocked himself by moaning instead of speaking.

Caleb's response was the sexiest smile he'd ever seen.

"You're right to be concerned," Caleb continued. "But I at least want to take the chance. If nothing else, we take from now through the off-season to figure us out. At most, I've only got eight or ten weeks left."

Aaron found his voice again. "The way you guys are playing, I think you'll be going far."

How was he talking hockey? Aaron needed to put a stop to this, but he lost himself in Caleb's eyes and in being this close to him. Yesterday's moment hadn't lasted very long at all, but Caleb showed no sign of letting him go today.

"The off-season will still be at least three months that I can be up here almost full-time, plus you'll be out of school."

"I don't know how I'm supposed to say anything when my mind can't focus."

"No one said I'd play fair in trying to get you to say yes."

"If only I had a penalty box handy." Aaron smirked at Caleb.

The low hum that came from Caleb seemed to vibrate

through Aaron. He loved the reaction his words had on Caleb.

"I think someone likes that." Aaron ran his tongue along Caleb's jawline again, and Caleb swayed a little bit as his hum turned more into a growl. "And that too."

"I like everything about you." Caleb's words weren't clear as Aaron kept distracting him with his tongue.

Aaron was past the point of no return. This was going to happen. Even if this was their only moment, at least it'd be a red-hot memory.

"Come on." Aaron extracted himself from Caleb's hug but grabbed his hand. "Let's go." Caleb repeatedly kissed Aaron's hand as he guided them toward the bedroom.

SIXTEEN

CALEB WAS ABOUT to fly apart at the seams. Aaron Price was leading him to his bedroom in a move that would either help cement the idea that they should have a go at being a couple, or would end up being a memory of something that couldn't be.

The combination of nerves and raw sexual excitement seized him, and yet he wanted to make sure this was good for Aaron. He knew Aaron was even more anxious about this than he was, and he wanted to ease that apprehension.

In the bedroom, the sheets were still askew from where Aaron had slept the night before. Caleb thought it was cute even as Aaron hustled over to the bed to straighten it out.

Caleb came up behind him to stop him. "We're just going to mess it up again." He gently turned Aaron to face him and kissed him again. He was so hungry for the kisses that he wasn't sure if he actually needed anything else. The first few from Aaron were so good, he knew he could go for a long time just getting to know his lips.

Caleb stole glances at Aaron. His eyes sparkled with an

intensity that fueled Caleb. Other times they were closed as Aaron seemed to relish the pleasure of the moment.

The exploration continued as Caleb felt Aaron in ways he hadn't been comfortable doing before. His physique was tight. He squeezed the lean muscles under the T-shirt on Aaron's arms and shoulders. He could tell Aaron stayed in shape.

Caleb reached for the hem of Aaron's tee and lifted it. They paused kissing just long enough for him to get it over Aaron's head. Caleb couldn't decide what to do next. He wanted more contact, but he also wanted to take in what he'd just uncovered. Smiling, he ran his hands down Aaron's smooth chest, letting one thumb brush a nipple and making Aaron flinch and giggle as if it tickled. He had just a bit of definition at his pecs and biceps, with gentle rises in his chest and arms.

"If you're just going to stare, I think I should have something to look at too." With no hesitation, Aaron got Caleb's sweatshirt over his head.

Aaron's breath caught as he did exactly what Caleb had done, feeling up his chest. "Is it embarrassing to say that I've wondered for a long time what you looked like without a shirt on?"

"A little bit, for me, anyway," Caleb said softly. "It's nothing special."

"You're so wrong. These muscles and abs, they're so perfect. It's like you're sculpted." Aaron continued to caress his skin. Aaron leaned in and, sounding breathless, ran his tongue along the contours of Caleb's pecs, and Caleb shuddered under the touch.

"Aaron." The name was drawn out, almost buried in a sigh of pleasure.

"You've got these perfect ridges too." Caleb ran a finger

along Aaron's pecs, down his torso's center line, and then off to the V that went into Aaron's pants. "You've no idea how sexy this line right here is." Caleb dropped to a squat and kissed along the V, first on the left side and then the right. On the right, however, instead of stopping at the waistband, he pulled the sweats down so he could continue, unveiling the top of Aaron's thatch of dark hair sitting above his cock. He stopped short of revealing that, though, content for the moment, and nibbled his way to Aaron's stomach, chest, neck, and ultimately back to his mouth.

"Oh my God. I didn't know it could be like this." Aaron pulled Caleb close so their chests pressed together. Caleb shivered at the feel of Aaron's protruding hard-on as it collided with his own.

"Like what?" Caleb asked.

"How right this feels."

Caleb stole a few kisses as he ran his thumbs over Aaron's hardened nipples.

Aaron shuddered, which triggered another rumbling moan from Caleb. "Two can play that game."

Aaron knew how to use his tongue, and it shook Caleb to his core every time. No one had done that to him before. He'd had his beard nuzzled and his neck kissed and licked, but something about what Aaron did sent shockwaves through him.

Caleb gently pushed Aaron onto the queen-sized bed and dropped down on him, putting most of his weight onto him. "This okay?"

"Oh my God, yes!"

Since Caleb was about a half foot taller, he adjusted so his mouth was aligned with Aaron's so they could kiss. He wanted to make sure they were perfectly situated. As they kissed, Aaron caressed Caleb's lower back, reaching inside the waistband of Caleb's jeans to feel up his ass.

"I think it might be time to lose the pants," Caleb said. "If that's okay with you."

Aaron nodded urgently.

"Don't move." Caleb pushed off the bed, and Aaron propped himself up on his elbows so he could watch. Caleb toed off his sneakers and then unbuttoned his jeans.

"You don't have to go so fast."

Caleb took the hint and slowed down even though he really wanted to dive in and get his body against Aaron's. He took his time to open the front of his jeans to reveal striped briefs in various shades of red. "Good?" Caleb inched his jeans down, leaving the briefs in place.

"You fill those out very well."

A little heat filled Caleb's cheeks as he looked down to see the very defined bulge of his cock running along the edge of the waistband.

"You're one to talk." Caleb reached over Aaron's legs and grabbed the clear tent in Aaron's sweats. "I think you're going commando, and that's very sexy."

They took a moment to gaze at each other. The sexy, fiery look in Aaron's eyes was so hot. Caleb liked that he'd inspired it. He wanted to see it every day.

"You gonna drop those or do I need to check you into the wall to make that happen?" Aaron sat up, crossing his legs under him.

"You told me to wait." Caleb put his hands on his hips and cocked his head as if confused.

"Well, now I want those off."

Caleb wasted no time dropping the briefs and freeing his cock. Aaron licked his lips as he unfolded his legs, leaned back, and raised his hips. Caleb didn't need instruction. He stepped forward and pulled the sweats off. As he'd suspected, Aaron wore nothing else, and his dick popped straight up. While they were of similar length, Aaron had more girth than Caleb, and it made his mouth water.

Caleb stretched over Aaron and again ran his tongue along the left side of the V. He started above the waist, and the lower he went, the more he expertly used his tongue to pleasure Aaron. Sometimes he'd stop and suck too. Aaron quivered as Caleb got closer to his throbbing cock.

He followed the V line along the ridge where Aaron's leg connected to his hip and right on to Aaron's balls, which were hanging loose between his spread legs. He nuzzled his nose into Aaron's ball sac and tasted the soft skin. Aaron softly moaned above him, persuading Caleb to keep going.

"I really need your dick in my mouth, please." Aaron's breathless request made Caleb's cock pulsate between his legs.

"Yes, sir, Mr. Price." Caleb's voice was partially obscured as he continued to nuzzle between Aaron's legs.

Aaron tensed up, and the encouraging noises trailed off. Caleb felt the anxiety in Aaron's legs, which were on either side of his head. He noted that the *sir* thing must not have been appreciated. He repositioned himself while continuing to explore Aaron's body with his mouth. He ultimately got his cock near Aaron's mouth as requested.

Caleb went down on Aaron's cock, hoping that would help recapture the mood. He took all of Aaron in one gulp. Aaron gasped as Caleb worked his tongue over Aaron's shaft. The plan seemed to work as the moans returned, stronger than before.

"Oh, Caleb. That's... so... good." Aaron could barely speak as his cockhead pushed against the back of Caleb's throat. "And these legs... my God, they're perfect."

Aaron kissed around Caleb's cock, not yet taking it in even as its hardness pressed against his face. Caleb hummed his pleasure as he continued to suck Aaron's cock. He loved the mouthful Aaron was, and how good he tasted as the occasional bit of precum dripped out. Carefully, Caleb caressed other areas of Aaron—legs, balls, stomach—with his free hand while the other kept his weight mostly off Aaron.

Aaron explored too, and Caleb almost choked from a pleasure overload when Aaron shifted from his balls to the space between them and his hole. What had been moans turned to whimpers as Aaron hit the tender skin with his tongue, leaving Caleb's cock to be teased just slightly by the whiskers on Aaron's chin. Without saying anything, Aaron pushed himself up just enough so his tongue could dart around Caleb's hole.

Caleb was forced to let go of Aaron's cock so he could breathe. He gripped the bedspread as waves of unprecedented pleasure crashed through him. He pushed his ass back onto Aaron's tongue as Aaron spread Caleb's cheeks to give himself better access. Caleb could do nothing but shudder and make guttural sounds. He wasn't prepared for Aaron to be such a pro at rimming. He did an incredible job. Caleb struggled to hold himself up as his arms started to shake.

Suddenly, Aaron stopped. "Okay, big boy. Here we go."

Caleb couldn't believe how easily Aaron rolled them over so he was suddenly on top. Before Caleb could say a word, Aaron moved off the bed to stand at the foot, where Caleb's legs now hung off. Caleb watched with anticipation as Aaron lifted his legs so his ass was in the air. Aaron then dove right back into the rim job, causing Caleb to cry out in ecstasy.

Caleb hadn't expected Aaron to be so aggressive. He liked it—a lot. He was usually the one in control because it was what was expected. And frankly, it was in his nature. While he'd started this, he was wildly turned on that Aaron had taken over and was driving him insane. No one had worked his ass like that, and while he wanted to know what Aaron's tongue could do to his cock, he didn't want to stop what was happening.

"Aaron... my God." Caleb's voice was strained and broken with whimpers as the stunning assault on his ass continued.

Aaron reached around and gently stroked Caleb's cock, which only made him vibrate more.

"Careful. You're gonna make me blow if you keep that up."

Aaron slowed the stroking, but the tongue action continued. He adjusted perfectly to Caleb's desires.

Caleb needed Aaron. Needed him right now. He shifted to the side, and while Aaron briefly whimpered in protest, Caleb scrambled to get in front of him and kiss him. It was an intense, passion-filled kiss that Aaron matched. They grabbed on to each other, pressing as much of their bodies together as possible.

"Please tell me you've got stuff here." Caleb's voice was muffled between kisses.

Aaron nodded and went to the nightstand. He quickly pulled out lube but then shuffled around in the drawer.

Caleb got off the bed and came up behind him, peppering his neck and shoulders with kisses as his erection poked Aaron's buttcheeks. "You've got a lot of toys," Caleb said, perching his head on Aaron's shoulder and looking into the drawer.

"I've been running solo for a while now." Aaron pulled a chain of condoms from the drawer.

"Give me those," Caleb said eagerly. He was happy to take back control, as he couldn't wait anymore. Caleb turned Aaron around and pushed him gently backward. He fell onto the bed and pushed himself so he was all on the bed. Caleb got next to him, ripped the condom open, and started rolling it down Aaron's cock.

"What're you doing?" There was no mistaking the surprise in Aaron's voice.

Caleb froze as he was about to lube Aaron up. "You can't get me worked up like that and then not let me ride on this dick." He squeezed it for emphasis. "I want it." He watched confusion cross Aaron's face. They studied each other, and Caleb looked for signs he was doing the wrong thing again, but a slight smile played across Aaron's lips, and that made Caleb tingle inside.

He got back to work lubing Aaron's thick cock before he straddled him. Caleb grabbed Aaron's legs and pulled them closer to his body. Aaron ran his hands over Caleb's quads as Caleb lubed himself and rocked back onto Aaron's cock.

He controlled himself so he didn't try to sit right down Aaron's rock-hard pole. It'd been a while since he'd been fucked. He vibrated as intense sensations rolled through him. Despite his anticipation of what was to come, he made sure to savor the moment.

"Holy fuck, you're big." Caleb looked down and saw fire in Aaron's eyes that sent jolts through him as if he were being touched.

He pushed down and growled as he forced himself to relax, taking some deep breaths. Suddenly, Aaron was inside, and Caleb gasped as pleasure and pain gripped him. "Gimme a second."

"Take your time." Aaron caressed Caleb's chest.

Caleb closed his eyes, concentrating. Aaron flicked at his nipples, and that was just the coaxing he needed.

"And you're so tight."

Caleb opened his eyes to find Aaron's eyes closed, but there was a goofy smile on his face. He clenched his ass a couple of times, squeezing Aaron's dick as hard as he could.

"My God. So good."

Caleb leaned down, making sure Aaron didn't slip out. His lips crashed into Aaron's for the hungriest kisses they'd traded yet as Caleb slowly moved himself along the shaft buried deep inside him.

Eventually, Caleb sat up and picked up the pace of the thrusts. Using his well-trained legs, he rode Aaron, leaving him nothing to do but moan and writhe under him. Caleb was the louder one, as he got Aaron deeper into his ass. They were covered with a sheen of sweat when Aaron matched Caleb's rhythm to push in farther.

"That's it. Right there," Caleb said as they worked together to keep hitting *that* spot.

Aaron grabbed hold of Caleb's cock, which had been bobbing against his stomach, and jerked it. Caleb had been leaking for some time, his cock slick and hard. Caleb clenched Aaron's cock tighter as Aaron worked his throbbing dick.

Without warning, Caleb's breath caught as he shot white ropes of cum across Aaron's chest and chin. Aaron went over the edge as Caleb's orgasm caused his hole to tighten. They both cried out.

Caleb slowly leaned over and gently kissed Aaron as he slid off his cock. Aaron whimpered a bit as he slipped out but didn't stop the kisses.

"That was amazing," Caleb eventually said, his face just inches from Aaron's.

"I don't think I can move."

Caleb carefully climbed off Aaron and collapsed next to him. He nestled close to Aaron, using Aaron's arm as a pillow. "I don't think we have to."

They lay there quietly, periodically touching and caressing one another, until they drifted off.

SEVENTEEN

AARON WOKE UP WITH A START, not realizing where he was at first. "Sorry!"

Something wasn't right. He had to get up, but an arm over his chest and a leg over his trapped him in place.

"What's wrong?" A man's voice... Caleb's voice, sounding groggy.

Caleb moved off him, and Aaron immediately missed the reassuring contact of Caleb's body so close to his.

"Caleb. Sorry," Aaron whispered, closing his eyes, wishing he could be anywhere but here. It was completely embarrassing waking up next to Caleb, practically screaming.

"It's okay." Caleb peppered kisses along Aaron's shoulder. "What are you apologizing for?"

"Nothing. I forgot where I was. It's been—" Aaron needed to stop talking. He'd only dig a deeper hole if he babbled on. He shook, and not from cold. Caleb in his bed was the last thing he should've allowed, but his resistance had crumbled. It'd been amazing, but the awkward part was on its way. And then what?

"You're shaking. Aaron, talk to me."

Aaron rolled off the bed. "It's probably better if you go. I... I've got class to prepare for and—"

"What?"

The look of hurt on his face stabbed at Aaron's heart. The furrowed brow, the confusion—it was something he never wanted to see on Caleb, especially if he was the cause.

"Look, you and me, it won't work out. I'm not right for you. You need more than just a schoolteacher. We both know that." Aaron turned to the bed where Caleb sat, the covers tangled around his waist so his chiseled chest was on display. It'd be too easy to fall back in with him and allow Caleb to do whatever he wanted.

"I don't understand. I thought we were going to figure this out together. How can you possibly know we won't work out?"

Aaron turned away, suddenly very aware that he stood naked in front of Caleb. Embarrassed heat rose in him as he thought about his very average body in front of Caleb's handsome, athletic form. He couldn't even think about what he'd allowed to happen earlier since it was something that should've stayed as a fantasy. He had to say something, anything, to get Caleb out of his apartment.

He steadied himself with a hand on the dresser across from his bed. "I can't do this."

Behind him, he heard Caleb shuffle out of bed. Instead of getting dressed, he spun Aaron around by the shoulder to face him. Aaron struggled to keep his emotions in check as they stood naked, face to face. He could crumble later. If he did that now, Caleb wouldn't go.

"Talk. To. Me." Caleb's confusion and hurt tore at Aaron's resolve. "I don't understand."

Aaron looked away, but Caleb gently brought his face back so their gazes met. Neither spoke. There was so much to tell, but saying it to Caleb didn't seem right.

"I can't," Aaron finally said.

Caleb put his hands at Aaron's waist. Their nakedness was distracting, and Aaron didn't appreciate his body betraying him, his cock already semi-erect. It'd be so easy to cast aside the doubt and just pull Caleb back to bed. That would also be the worst possible move.

"Sure you can. We've known each other long enough that you can tell me anything." His voice was soft, soothing, and caused a new wave of emotions to well up that Aaron struggled to keep at bay.

It took some time before he answered. He wanted to make sure he kept his voice even. "Not even Pam knows the whole story."

Caleb let out a small sigh that Aaron didn't know what to make of. When Caleb stepped back, Aaron thought he'd finally made his point. Caleb found his red striped underwear on the floor and put them on, but then instead of getting his jeans, he grabbed Aaron's sweats and handed them to him.

When Aaron didn't take them, Caleb extended them a second time. "Put these on and tell me what's wrong."

Reluctantly, Aaron slipped them on and allowed Caleb to lead him back to the bed, where he pulled him down onto the mattress. Caleb settled against the headboard, sitting up, while Aaron sat with his legs folded under him, looking at Caleb. Aaron didn't know what to do. Part of him wanted Caleb desperately. Another part needed Caleb to leave so he could spare himself the pain of having to be truthful about what happened in Los Angeles.

"Please, Aaron." Caleb's concerned gaze never left Aaron, but Aaron couldn't look him in the eye.

Instead, he focused on the stream of light coming through the curtains from the window adjacent to the bed. "There's more to why I came home than just needing a job. That part is true. There were budget cuts and I was let go, but I could've probably found something else out there. It was...." Aaron steeled himself. "I was seeing a guy, for a few years and...."

Aaron despised the shake that rattled through him as he thought about Tyson. He'd worked hard to block out the memories. Just when he thought he was moving on, Caleb had shown up, and sometimes Aaron clearly heard Tyson's voice in his head telling him that he had nothing Caleb would want.

"It's okay." Caleb touched Aaron's knee, which was the only part of him in reach. "Did he do something to you? Hurt you?"

The concern in Caleb's voice almost did Aaron in. He wasn't sure he deserved the sentiment or the patience since he'd been the one to be so stupid.

"Physically, only once, and that was the end of it. I dealt with a lot, but no one gets to hit me."

Caleb hissed in what sounded like disgust, and Aaron flinched. He wasn't surprised Caleb wouldn't want to be with someone who'd allow himself to be hit. From the corner of his eye, he saw Caleb lean forward and reach for him, and he couldn't stop himself from jerking back. Caleb's hand stopped in midair.

"You have to know I wouldn't do that to you."

Aaron nodded and relaxed, which allowed Caleb to touch him. He gently pulled Aaron toward him and grace- fully maneuvered them so they lay next to each other with

Aaron nestled against Caleb's chest. Aaron took a deep breath and let his body mold itself to Caleb's. Even in the moment of vulnerability, he relished how safe he actually felt next to him.

"I'm sorry. I thought I was past all this."

Caleb hugged him tight. "I can't say I know what you went through, but you don't have to apologize for still having feelings about it. If anything, I'm sorry for dredging it up."

They lay quietly for a few minutes, Caleb holding him tightly. Aaron appreciated his patience. Not that he needed it, but it was more proof that Caleb was nothing at all like Tyson.

"I met—" Aaron paused to decide if he should use a name. Tyson still played baseball in Anaheim, and Aaron didn't want to stir up any trouble. "I met this guy in a gay bar in West Hollywood. It wasn't my usual haunt, but a friend was celebrating his birthday and there I was. I could tell by looking at the guy that he was an athlete and very much my type. He was handsome, charming. He seemed nice. We got to talking and hit it off, so we traded numbers. I should've known from the moment my calls went to voice-mail more often than not that something was up."

Relief and terror flooded through Aaron as he told the story for the first time.

"He was a professional athlete, a baseball player, and he wasn't out of the closet. He explained that it was important we be as discreet as possible until he could find the right time to publicly come out, which he assured me he was going to do... eventually. After we had been going out for three months, he finally admitted that he had a fiancée. I blew up at him for not being honest with me, that I was just something on the side. He fed me a story about breaking up with her and being with me. That I was the one he really loved. He said he needed to be his true self and he just needed time. I was a fucking idiot for believing him."

"Oh man. You really loved him."

Aaron couldn't decide if that was a statement or a question, but he kept going. "I did then. I wanted to be there for him. I knew all along that he wasn't out to his team, and I understood that. In the beginning, we had fun together. We'd go to these little out-of-the-way places that he knew, great little restaurants, places I suppose where they wouldn't ask questions about the baseball player and his 'friend.' There were even a few times I went with him when he played away games. He'd put me up at amazing hotels and sneak over to be with me at night. He'd always have to get back to the team hotel by sunrise, though.

"But that didn't last. He got more possessive and demanding—so paranoid of being found out that the only place we'd meet was my apartment. It felt like I just had a fuck buddy instead of a boyfriend. I suspected that he had other guys too. He showed me pictures on his phone once and he swiped into some of him with another guy in a hot tub. He tried to play it off that it was a teammate at some party. But he seemed very weird about it. As much as ballplayers travel, he could've had guys all over the place. I probably should've confronted him more about that, but I never did. I focused on what he always said—that he wanted me once he broke off his engagement."

He shifted slightly so he could look at Caleb, which suddenly seemed very important. "He got more defensive and hurtful as I tried to figure out what our future was. Over a few months, I let him convince me that I should lay off the questions and be happy that someone as famous as him showed an interest in someone like me in the first place.

And, of course, he knew how to apologize when his temper got the better of him. On our anniversary, I asked him when he was going to leave the girl, and he slapped me hard across the face. He called me an ungrateful bitch."

"How did you not call the police on his sorry ass?" Caleb sounded like he was ready to fight the one who'd hurt Aaron.

"I guess you could say the slap flipped a switch in me, made me realize the situation I was in was never going to get better. He was never going to break up with her. I'd never hit anyone in my life, but I gave him one hell of a shiner and told him that if he ever came to see me or called me again, I'd make sure his fiancée and the team found out about him. A couple of weeks after that, I learned I was out of a job. After months of him telling me that no one else would have me and then losing my teaching job, it was a hell of a blow. Pam offering me a position and coming back home to Foster Grove was the chance to start over."

Caleb was silent, and Aaron worried he'd said too much. On the other hand, Caleb hadn't moved and his expression hadn't really changed. Aaron had no idea what he was thinking.

"Is he the reason you're so resistant to starting something with me?"

Aaron couldn't decide where to look to keep his emotions in check. "My heart knows you could never be like him, but...." He took a deep breath to steady himself. "I'm skittish. I suppose I've made it worse on myself by not telling anyone, but it's humiliating. I should've known when to walk away."

Gently, Caleb guided Aaron's head to rest against his shoulder and kissed the top. "I'm glad you told me. It helps me understand why you tense up or seem sad. You have to know, *I* want you. I have since I was sixteen, and these past few days have shown me that's still true. You're worth doing whatever it takes to make you comfortable with *us*. You just have to tell me."

"You know there's a lot more stuff we need to work through, right?"

"I do."

"Let's not forget that you're a superstar. You're one of *the* faces of Rangers hockey, and the other guy was just an outfielder with an inflated ego and a crappy disposition. I'm still just a teacher from upstate New York. Do you really think people are going to accept that?"

"We're just two boys from Foster Grove who finally decided to give it a shot after years of dreaming about it. Who cares what people say? We're the only ones who count. And if you say no—" Caleb's chest rose and fell under Aaron—it didn't sound like a sigh; it was a deep, steadying breath. "If you ultimately decide no, I'll try to accept that. But let me show you what I already know—we'd be amazing together."

"Your enthusiasm is reassuring." Aaron pressed closer to Caleb.

"Good." He kissed the top of Aaron's head again. "You know you've got the perfect defender, right?"

"Really?" Aaron had no idea.

"Pam. She'll kick my ass if I hurt you."

"Oh yeah." Aaron laughed a little, which felt good. "That probably goes both ways."

"True."

Aaron pulled on Caleb's shoulders, and he lowered himself so they ended up lying together. Without a word, they wrapped themselves around each other and made out.

EIGHTEEN

WHAT DID YOU DO?

The voice in Aaron's head repeated that question over and over as soon as he left his apartment for work on Monday morning. He'd managed to stay in a cocoon with Caleb on Sunday. After Aaron unloaded his baggage, they'd spent the rest of the day exploring each other and eventually ordered dinner in. They stayed away from discussing anything that had to do with their future, which should've been their primary focus.

Then there was the sex.

The first round had been amazing, with the unexpected twist that he had fucked Caleb. When they got going for round two, Caleb took control, proving that he had grace and athletic prowess both on and off the ice. The way they connected, physically and emotionally, was unlike anything Aaron had ever experienced. Caleb had amazing technique. At one point, he had kept Aaron on edge for so long that when the two of them finally came together, it was like the world shattered into a million multicolored pieces before peacefully returning—whole, the two of them together.

Caleb stayed, and there was no denying Aaron enjoyed waking up next to him. They even left at the same time—Caleb for his morning workout and Aaron for school. It felt so natural, as if they'd always done it and always would.

Aaron's internal voice spoke up as soon as he was in the car alone. He'd really screwed up. His heart had betrayed his brain by discussing Tyson, which consequently brought him closer to Caleb.

Everything since their first dinner had been amazing. Reconnecting with Caleb. Discovering the attraction. He could be *the one*.

Aaron slammed his hand on his steering wheel as he sat at a red light. At what cost, though? This couldn't end well. Caleb was going back to New York in two days. His rehab time in Foster Grove was just that. Despite anything Caleb might have said on how it—they—*could* work, nothing was decided.

Aaron thought he was pretty good at being alone. He'd dated on and off before Tyson and understood balancing schedules, especially across the vast expanse that was LA where any relationship could feel long-distance simply because of the time it could take driving anywhere. Then Tyson came along and nudged him slowly into a corner. Aaron had let that happen; he couldn't allow that again. He was still working to get back to being okay. He trusted Caleb, but what feelings would be triggered while Caleb was traveling? It wasn't just road games that would keep Caleb away, though. They didn't even live in the same city.

As he pulled into the school parking lot, he struggled to stuff those feelings into a box because he couldn't fixate on any of this during the day. He had students to teach and some parents to meet with in the afternoon—meetings he should've prepped for yesterday but hadn't. That would have to get done during lunch.

Pam leaned against her car with a coffee in her hand and another on the hood.

She was early.

Despite starting the morning with Caleb, Aaron had arrived at school at his usual time, and it looked like she was going to take advantage of that.

"Shit," Aaron whispered, even though he was alone in the car. This would be about the picture. He'd had a dozen missed calls and texts from her yesterday. Caleb and Aaron had turned off their phones so they wouldn't hear the new notifications while they were together. In hindsight, it was foolish, a childish attempt to keep the real world at bay.

He steeled himself, then grabbed his messenger bag from the passenger seat and got out of the car. "Good morning," he said, trying desperately to sound normal as he walked over to Pam, who didn't move.

"Is it? I talked to Caleb yesterday about the picture, and he said he was going to see you. After that I couldn't get in touch with either one of you. The only reason I didn't crash your door down is because Caleb's car was parked in front of your apartment when I came over." She handed over the coffee. "Care to explain?"

He took the coffee, the to-go cup warm in his hand. "I don't even know where to start." They turned toward the school, which was still quiet, as students weren't expected to arrive and start the day for another thirty minutes.

"Let's begin with this: Are you okay?"

"Yes. No. I don't know. It wasn't supposed to go this far."

"Please tell me you guys talked." They walked up the

front steps and through the main doors of the school as they chatted.

"We did... a little. There's a lot more we need to sort out." He sounded like a child trying not to admit to doing something wrong. "It was a perfect day, though." He smiled what he thought might have been his biggest smile in months. "Initially, he came over to talk about the picture and to make sure I was okay with it being out there. We talked about a lot of things, including what might be possible for us. And he stayed over, which was really good."

She nodded, and Aaron was thankful she had the good sense not to press for details.

"So, you two are going to be a thing?" she asked, her tone hopeful.

Once in Aaron's classroom, they ended up in their usual coffee talk positions. "He says we should try to figure things out as we go. I think we're going to end up hurting each other because I want what I can't have."

"You can have anything you want."

"You know what I mean."

"Actually, I don't. I think it's all false obstacles." Pam didn't often take her serious tone with him. Even though she was just trying to help, it only stressed him out more.

"You don't know that!" he insisted emphatically, louder than he intended. "He's a pro athlete, traveling for weeks on end. Beyond that, we don't live in the same city, so it's not like he'd be coming home to me. And that picture is proof of it. People kiss in that park all the time and don't end up trending on Twitter. That would become my reality. And there are—"

He stopped before he said more. It had been difficult enough discussing Tyson with Caleb; he wasn't going to open up about that right before he had to teach.

146

"Don't be stubborn," she said when Aaron didn't finish. "If you both want it, and it sounds like you do, figure out what it takes." Her phone chirped and she sighed. "I've got to get to a disciplinary meeting. See you at lunch?"

He shook his head. "Can't. I've got to prep for some parent meetings. After that, Caleb's picking me up for hockey practice."

She gave him a slight nod that he knew was a sign of her approval. "If you need to talk later, you know how to find me."

"Thanks."

Pam left and Aaron unpacked his bag. At least the class plans for today were ready. He flipped his tablet to the document that detailed what he needed to write on the board.

"Mr. Price?" It was Catherine, sounding way too excited, as she stood at the classroom door. "Is it true about you and Mr. Carter? I saw the picture of you two kissing." She giggled as she said the last word.

More students came in as she approached his desk at the front of the classroom.

"You didn't tell us he was your boyfriend," Charlie chimed in before Aaron could respond.

"My dad said that was wrong," Ben offered.

The rest of his class filed in and gathered around Aaron's desk. He faced them as the questions kept coming.

"Are you going to get married?"

"Oh, are you going to have kids too?"

"They can't have kids."

"My uncles adopted a baby girl. Why can't they have a baby?"

This was not a discussion he wanted to have, but the students talked over one another. He had to take control of the situation. "Class!" Aaron shouted over the din. "Put your things away and take your seats."

"But the bell hasn't rung yet," Charlie said.

Thankfully, it sounded just as Charlie had finished his sentence. "Please take your seats so we can get started."

The class grumbled as they hung up their coats and got settled at their desks.

Aaron quickly went through roll call just in time for the morning announcements. Then it was time for their version of Monday show-and-tell.

"Okay." Aaron sat on the edge of his desk. "Who wants to tell us what they did this weekend?" Several hands shot up. "Maggie." He pointed to the girl in the third row of desks.

"I saw your picture on TV while my brother was watching hockey. Are you going to go live in New York?"

Aaron stifled a sigh. He'd assumed most of his students —they were third graders, after all—wouldn't have caught the picture. He hadn't thought about it being on TV, though. It was a bigger mess than he'd realized. Did Caleb know it was on TV? Maybe they shouldn't have unplugged yesterday. While Caleb had Grant to run interference for him, Aaron had no one.

"These are not questions for you to ask." Aaron used his authoritative teacher's voice. "Remember how we've talked about things that are personal, and it's important to be polite and not ask questions about those things?"

Many of the students nodded.

"This is one of those things. It was wrong of the person who took the picture to invade our privacy—do you know what privacy is?"

Charlie's hand went up, and Aaron nodded. "My sister

says I invade hers when I'm in her room if she hasn't invited me."

"That's a perfect example, Charlie."

"But you were in the park where everyone could see."

"Yes, we were. It still doesn't mean it's okay that someone snapped and posted the picture without our permission. It's not against the law, but it's still not polite."

Maggie raised her hand again.

"Yes."

"But you haven't said if you were going to move."

"I'm not going to move. You can't get rid of me that easily." He laughed a little, and the class snickered along with him. "You know Mr. Carter and I have been friends for a long time. He has to go back to New York and his team this week. He has to do his job, and I have to do mine here with you." Aaron hoped that would put an end to the matter, at least for the time being. "Now, let's talk about your weekend. Maggie, do you actually have something?"

She came up to the front of the room and talked about going with her mother to a plant store—which Aaron told the class was called a nursery—and then she helped do some early planting. She thought it would've been gross to dig in the dirt, but she kind of enjoyed it.

Four others talked about their weekends, and Aaron felt pretty good that any questions about him and Caleb were safely on the back burner.

Though if his kids had all these questions, he could only imagine what the rest of the world was thinking.

NINETEEN

AARON WAS glad he had a couple of parent meetings that afternoon since it meant almost everyone was gone before Caleb would stop by the school to drive them to the rink. Why wasn't he just driving his own car? It had seemed cute at the time to be chauffeured, but did he really want to show up at practice with Caleb, all eyes on the two of them?

Caleb smiled when Aaron got in the car, and Aaron couldn't hold back a smile. Caleb had a knack for melting any resistance he had.

"How was your day?"

Aaron leaned back against the seat and sighed. "Exhausting." He closed his eyes and was startled when Caleb took his hand.

"I'm sorry. I imagine I was a large part of that."

"*We* were a large part of that. We were both in that photo, kissing where anyone could see. It's the first thing the kids hit me with this morning. Actually, it started with Pam in the parking lot."

"Yeah, I called her this morning. I think I got a good

taste of what she's like as a principal. Told me I had a lot of nerve not answering my phone."

"Exactly. It's been nuts with questions that just keep coming from everyone. How do you deal with it?"

Caleb shrugged guiltily before he chuckled. "I leave Grant to sort it out. He says most of the response is positive, including the reaction to my statement that we'd like to be left alone so we can figure out what our future might be."

He said *might*. Was he having second thoughts? Or just saying that to keep the public at bay? Or maybe he didn't want to pressure Aaron.

"I'm not sorry we did it," Caleb continued. "Or for the incredible day we spent together."

"Me either." It was true; Aaron wasn't the least bit sorry. "But what happens now?"

Caleb pulled out of the parking lot. "I got confirmation this morning that I'm headed back to New York. I'm expected at the doctor's on Wednesday morning, so I'll drive down tomorrow evening."

Aaron's heart ached, but he managed a nod and to sound composed. "I know the team will be happy to have you back, especially with playoffs starting Friday."

"I'd be lying if I said I wasn't looking forward to being back with them."

"And your life, I'd imagine."

Caleb was silent as he drove. Aaron wasn't sure what it meant that he wasn't even stealing occasional glances at him.

At a red light, Caleb faced Aaron. "I like life here too—with you. These glimpses of us being a couple." Caleb's pained expression wasn't lost on Aaron.

"How do we make that work? After a handful of get-togethers that we haven't really called dates, can we make a commitment to a relationship?"

"We're both going to be off soon. You'll have summer break and my season will be over—we'll have time." The cars behind them honked since Caleb missed the green light. As he returned his focus to the road, he continued to talk. "It'll be a time to settle into a routine and go on all the dates we want."

"A routine that'll be broken as soon as fall starts." Aaron wasn't trying to be cynical, just realistic as he looked at Caleb while trying not to look or sound defeated.

Caleb opened his mouth and then closed it.

"What?"

"Nothing." Caleb tried to shrug it off.

"The last thing we should do at this point is hide things from each other."

"I was going to suggest that you could take a year off because I could easily support the both of us."

"That's not going to happen." He sounded more defensive than he meant to. "I realize we'll never be equal, in a lot of ways. But not only do I want to contribute to any relationship I'm in, I also love my job."

"I know. That's why I didn't want to say it."

The problem was that he thought it. Aaron didn't want to be a kept man, or a house husband, or whatever.

They were quiet as they continued to the rink. When they arrived, Caleb parked. Aaron put his hand on Caleb's shoulder and felt the tension quickly release.

"Sorry." Caleb's voice was low even though they were still in the car. "I know we need a serious talk. Pam gave me my marching orders on that."

Aaron nodded. "I got that too."

"We've got to do this thing. We'll talk after, okay? Either your place or mine so we're in private."

Aaron agreed. "Are you going to say anything to the kids about going to New York?"

"Of course. It's in the news."

"And you don't want to just... disappear."

"No. I couldn't do that to the kids."

Caleb squeezed Aaron's knee before they got out of the SUV and grabbed skates and Caleb's other gear from the back. It tugged on Aaron's heart to see his skates jumbled up with Caleb's. He wanted that for his life more than he cared to admit—even to himself.

The ninety minutes of practice dragged on. Caleb was an ace at talking with the kids about his upcoming return to New York, and he promised to come back in the summer to work with the team for a couple of weeks. Caleb even firmly, but gently, addressed the picture when one of the players asked about it.

"That's not a topic for here, and neither Coach Aaron or myself will discuss it. So please respect that."

There were a couple murmurs of disappointment, but no one pressed. Aaron braced for Ian's questions, but he said nothing. He committed Caleb's words to memory so he could use them if necessary.

Once practice wrapped, Caleb took Aaron back to the school parking lot to get his car and then meet him at Aaron's place. He wasn't sure it was the best plan since it was where so much had happened yesterday, but it was closer to the school so they'd start the talk sooner here.

Once they were inside, they stood, not even removing their jackets.

"I don't know what to do," Aaron finally said.

"I know what I want to do, but it's probably not what you're looking for."

Aaron sighed, closed his eyes, and dropped his head, his chin resting on his chest. He was sure Caleb was talking about a kiss or maybe more. It was the wrong answer, but just the thought of it made Aaron tingle inside.

"I want it," Aaron whispered, his heart betraying him. "But there's so much to sort out before we get deeper into it."

"Isn't that part of it, though? The more we fall for each other, the harder it will be to break us apart."

"It's got to be more than sex, though." Aaron moved to put some distance between him and Caleb so he wouldn't just throw himself on him.

"Isn't it already? We've got years of history. It's not like we're strangers."

Caleb slipped out of his jacket and hung it on one of the hooks by the door. He swiftly stepped behind Aaron and removed his to hang it up. "I don't want to make this more complicated." Caleb gestured toward the living room, his gentlemanly nature coming through again. "And I know it is. I've heard what you said—what you need. I don't know how to make that happen, at least not right now. But I'm stubborn and want to figure it out."

"I'm not sure that's possible," Aaron said as he entered the living room. "We've got very different lives, live in different places, and you know I've got a ton of baggage."

Caleb went on to the kitchen, adding to the feeling that he lived there already, and returned quickly with two bottles of water. Before he delivered a bottle to Aaron, he stopped short. "Wow," he said softly. "You kept it."

Aaron didn't have to guess what he was talking about. "I told you I always remembered it."

Caleb put the water down on top of the short bookshelf that was behind the couch and then picked up the "World's Best Tutor" trophy and examined it. "I had no idea you'd kept it all this time."

Aaron met Caleb's gaze. "It was important. It came from you."

"See?" Caleb said, setting the trophy carefully back in place. "You've waited years for this, and so have I. Let's see what we can make of it."

"That's not fair. It's different—a schoolboy crush and an adult relationship."

Caleb sighed while Aaron pushed his hands through his hair.

"What's not fair is that you're not even thinking about ways we can be together. You're just shutting it down. I'm willing to fight for us. Aren't you?"

Everything Caleb said was reasonable, but Aaron couldn't help but remember what it was like with Tyson as they settled into their routine. Come September, he'd hardly see Caleb and might not even hear from him regularly.

Caleb came up behind Aaron, who stood at the window that looked out on the building's small yard and parking lot. "Will you at least think seriously about this, and we can talk while I'm away?"

"All I do is think about us." Aaron fixed his gaze across the street, trying not to focus on the reflection of him and Caleb in the glass.

Caleb began peppering Aaron's neck with kisses.

"That doesn't help," Aaron said, even though he didn't move to stop him.

"I'll do anything to make the case that we should try for this, including seduction." Caleb spun Aaron around so he could kiss him on the mouth. It didn't take long for Aaron to surrender despite the voices in his head telling him to stop.

There were no more protests. They spent the night wrapped around each other with no talk about the future. There was sex and some dinner cobbled together out of what was in Aaron's kitchen. Aaron didn't know if Caleb felt the same somberness he did, but like the future, it was something he didn't mention. He simply made sure to ignore his common sense and enjoy time with Caleb for one more night.

TWENTY

It wasn't surprising that the team doctor and physical therapist put Caleb through his paces. If his foot hadn't healed right, he could be in a lot of pain once it was under the stress of game play or, even worse, prone to breaking again. Wednesday morning was filled with x-rays, scans, and tests.

Ultimately, the doc said it looked great and his range of motion was even better than expected. Caleb got the approval to return to the team immediately.

He couldn't remember a time he dreaded getting back on the ice more.

When he'd broken his arm in fifth grade, it scared him to go back on the ice because he thought it'd happen again. By the time he was in middle school, that kind of fear didn't get to him. He always wanted right back in the game.

This time it was like a punishment, taking care of the administrative stuff and meeting with Coach, because his heart was in Foster Grove. There was no going back, though. He'd skate with the team Thursday and Friday morning, so he'd be ready for game one of the playoffs on

Friday night. At least with the game on Friday, he could invite Aaron to come down to watch and, if he was lucky, stay the weekend.

Caleb's next stop was to see Dimitri. He'd hoped Dimitri would be content hanging out at his place, but he wanted to go out and Caleb wanted to talk—so out it was. They met up at one of Dimitri's favorite bars in Hell's Kitchen, where at least it was quiet this early in the evening.

Caleb spotted Dimitri on one of the small couches in a back corner that gave him a good view of the entire place. He'd already attracted the attention of a young and very tattooed man. Dimitri at least looked up when Caleb came in. They traded a nod of acknowledgment before Caleb went to the bar to get a beer. Hopefully, Dimitri could dispatch with his fan before he came back.

Dimitri stood as Caleb approached and embraced him in a hug. "It's good to see you. What's the word?"

Tattoo Guy was still on the couch, looking expectant, and that made Caleb uncomfortable. He kept his focus on Dimitri. "Back at practice tomorrow and in the game Friday."

"Thank God. I didn't like the idea of going into the playoffs without you. This is Peter," Dimitri said, indicating the man on the couch. Caleb gave a nod. "Peter, this is Caleb, the teammate I told you I was meeting. Can we catch up later?"

"I wouldn't mind *catching up* with both of you," he said, cocking his eyebrow in what Caleb assumed was supposed to be a flirtatious expression.

Thankfully, Dimitri quickly put an end to that idea. "I'm afraid that's not going to happen."

Peter got up. "Well, if you change your mind, I'll be around."

Dimitri grabbed his beer bottle off the low table as he watched Peter saunter to the bar. "He might be too much work. Although those tats...." He made a growling sort of noise. "I'd love to see the rest."

"I've missed hanging out with you."

"Here's to at least eight or nine more weeks of being together." Dimitri clanked his bottle against Caleb's, and they both sat. Caleb sighed. "That's not exactly the reaction someone trying to win a Stanley Cup is supposed to have."

"I know." Caleb pulled on the beer bottle's label so he wouldn't have to look at his friend. "My body's ready to go, but I've got to get my head in it. I'm sure getting on the ice tomorrow will do the trick, being back out there with you and the rest of the team."

"This is about what's his name, isn't it?"

"Aaron," Caleb was quick to add.

"Yeah, Aaron." Dimitri nodded. "How did he get such a hold on you so fast? You hardly take a sick day. You come in and cough all over the rest of us because you want to play so bad. When you broke your foot, you did everything you could to persuade Doc to wrap it and let you play the next day, even though it was your third break. Suddenly, you have to find a way to get your head in the game? Is he some kind of witch who's put a spell on you?"

"If you met him, you'd understand. Maybe after Friday's game. I'm hoping he'll come down."

"What?" Dimitri's surprise took Caleb aback. "You're asking the distraction to come here? You've got it bad."

"I've had a thing for him for... forever, it seems like. Now that I know he feels the same, I can't let that go easily. It's incredible to watch him work with his students. He actually likes hockey. He's smart. Maybe too smart, really. He can't see a way for us to work."

"Or maybe he knows enough to get that you can't be tied down—at least not right now."

"I'm not you, D."

"That's not what I mean. This isn't the easiest life to maintain a relationship of any kind. We see that all the time with guys who break up or get divorced. Why do you want to add that stress and distraction, especially during the playoffs?"

Caleb took a long pull on his beer. "Oh, come on. We know plenty of guys who make it work long-term." Caleb considered, only briefly, mentioning Aaron's previous heart-break and abuse but didn't because it wasn't his story to tell. "I don't have any answers for you, just like I don't for him. All I can say is that I want to give it a go. What would you do if you met someone?"

"I meet someone all the time. Spend a night or two, and then we go back to our lives."

"But you want more than a hookup someday, right?"

"Like what my mom and dad had where they were screaming at each other for years? No, thanks. Don't start that 'not everyone is like that.' I can't imagine a guy I'd want to settle with. It's too much fun seeing what's out there."

Caleb couldn't tell if Dimitri really felt that way or if he was just being difficult. "Well, I'm pretty sure I know who my guy is."

"I wish I had some advice." Dimitri reached out and grabbed some peanuts from the bowl on the small table in front of them. "What you're talking about is way outside my expertise."

"There's got to be something I can say to him that will prove this can all work. Or for him to at least take the leap. He's too worried about us getting hurt to even give it a try."

"He's got every reason to worry about that. What

happens when you meet someone on the road? Or a guy piques his interest while you're gone? Out of sight, out of mind?"

"Hang on. What makes you think I'd leave him for someone on the road?"

"Okay, someone here, in the city where you actually live."

"You know I'm not the kind of guy who fucks around."

"Fine, but imagine meeting a captivating random man, and rather than getting to go home to Aaron, you go to an empty apartment. It's the same for him up there."

"And yet we both have been living alone."

They sat quietly, drinking and watching the music videos that played on the flat screens over the bar. Caleb also caught the eye of Peter, the tattooed flirt, who seemed intent on waiting Dimitri out. He didn't know how Dimitri did what he did—the seemingly endless string of affairs that usually only burned hot for a few days, maybe a week at most, before fizzling out.

Dimitri finally spoke up. "I'm just going to tell you to do what I do. Follow your heart. If you want to make it work with Aaron, do it. My heart tells me to enjoy the variety that life has to offer and fuck around as much as possible. If I didn't do that, I'd go crazy. You'll be miserable if you don't do everything you can to bring him around."

"Maybe if he comes down for the weekend, he'll see that it can work."

"Try not to bring any of this drama onto the ice, though. We need you at your best."

"Yes, *Coach*." Caleb smirked at his friend.

"You wanna go to your place and play some video games? Take your mind off all this for a while?"

"Do you need to take tattoo guy somewhere?"

"He's being too clingy. He's watched us the whole time. Besides, my best friend needs me—unless...."

"Don't even say it. I do *not* need that. Beating you at *NHL 17* will be enough."

Dimitri stood and Caleb followed. "Let's go. And why do you think you're going to beat me anyway?"

"Because it's what happens when we're on Xbox."

"It could be different this time."

"Um, no."

They laughed as they headed out of the bar and grabbed a cab to go to Caleb's.

TWENTY-ONE

Aaron hadn't expected Caleb's invitation to come down to city to watch his first game back. His initial plan was to decline because there was no way he could get into the city in time after school. But Pam wouldn't let him hide behind that excuse and personally covered his class so he could hit the road. He played a mix of power ballads and dance tunes on the drive to keep him from thinking too much or getting too nervous.

He followed Grant's instructions on how to drop off his car at Caleb's building. It was a super fancy short glass tower on the Lower West Side. Aaron couldn't imagine what the inside must look like, but he'd know before the end of the night. The doorman took his keys so the car could be parked and arranged for his overnight bag to be taken up to Caleb's.

He wasn't used to so much help getting things done.

He arrived at Madison Square Garden right on time and texted Grant once he passed through security. The lobby in front of the ticket pickup windows was crowded as people spilled in from the security lines and scurried either to get tickets or go to their seat. It was the East Coast version of the Staples Center, where Aaron had been all of one time because Tyson took him to see some important college basketball game. He hadn't enjoyed it. This would be much better because it was Caleb playing.

Grant seemed to appear magically out of the crowd. "Hey, Aaron." He smiled as he shook Aaron's hand. "Good to see you. Any trouble getting here?"

"Pretty okay, actually. Traffic, of course, but Pam forced me out of school with more than enough time to get here."

"Excellent. So, you'll need this." He handed Aaron a couple of cards attached to a lanyard, similar to the ones Grant had around his neck. "These identify you as a VIP and get you access to the waiting room afterward. I'll make sure you get there, but they prove you belong if anyone checks."

Aaron put them over his head and looked at the cards, feeling a little awkward at receiving the specialized status. He followed Grant, keeping close to him. Instead of following the crowds, Grant took him through a door and down several hallways. It was a dizzying maze, and Aaron was glad he was with Grant, while at the same time, he hoped he wouldn't have to retrace this path.

"Caleb got a terrific seat for you." They emerged inside a nicely appointed lounge filled with people who seemed overdressed for the event—designer jeans, sweaters, and jackets. That left Aaron feeling way underdressed in a Rangers sweatshirt and jeans. He figured Caleb would just get him a regular seat where he'd blend in with the other fans. Maybe he should've asked what to wear? He didn't want to embarrass Caleb—or Grant, for that matter.

THE HOCKEY PLAYER'S HEART

They passed through the lounge and down to a seat just four rows off the ice, directly behind the New York bench.

Holy crap.

Caleb would be just a few feet away. This was unreal. Looking around The Garden, he expected to be up several levels. Up where the people were dressed like he was.

"This is pretty amazing," Aaron said.

"Right? You're here on the aisle. There are servers who can bring food to your seat, or you can go in the lounge and hang out, have food, whatever you want. It's all on the house —just show them your credentials."

"Okay."

"So, I need to go manage some pregame press for Caleb. I'll check on you periodically, and I'll come pick you up after the game and take you where you'll meet up with him and actually get on with your night."

"Okay."

Great. He was suddenly stuck with a single word in his vocabulary. How could Caleb think he belonged in this place? Everyone was going to know he'd accidentally slipped behind the velvet rope.

"And you've got my cell number. Call or text if you need anything. And, most important, have fun." Grant squeezed his shoulder and then was off like a shot.

Aaron fidgeted before the players came out for warmups. He read his phone. He looked around. He tried to feel like it was okay to be where he was. When Caleb came out onto the ice with the team, though, Aaron focused everything on number twenty-eight.

"Excuse me, sir." A deep, booming voice came from his right, and Aaron looked up. A hulking man in a black blazer, with a name tag that identified him as security, looked at him as if he was ready to pick him up and move him. "Are you in the correct section?"

This was the moment he'd get ejected from The Garden before he could watch Caleb play even a minute of the game.

"Yes. Yes, I am." He stood and held out his credentials from his body so they could be inspected.

The guard examined the cards and scanned one of them. "My apologies, Mr. Price. Enjoy the game." Without another word, the guard retreated back to the lounge.

Even though he was jittery, before he sat, he turned his back to the ice, pulled out his phone, and snapped a selfie.

Once comfortably ensconced in his seat, he typed to Pam. *Can you believe how close I am to the ice? OMG!*

He attached the picture and sent it. It only took less than a minute for the reply.

I hate you right now. Have fun!

Aaron forgot any issues he had about his seat once the game started. He only had eyes for Caleb, who more than once shot him a smile as he came to the bench—not always, but more than enough to warm Aaron's heart.

The game play was thrilling, and he freely leaped up to cheer Rangers goals and strong plays. He was also quick to boo anything good Boston did. The excitement took over.

Grant joined him for the third period since the three seats next to Aaron were empty, as were several others in the section. Apparently, the people who could afford tickets in this section liked to watch from the lounge area, where it was warmer.

As the clock wound down to only five minutes left, New York was up by a goal and pushing hard to secure the win. It had been a tight, back-and-forth game against Boston.

Aaron, Grant, and the rest of the crowd suddenly stood as Dimitri took off with the puck, followed closely by Caleb, who skated hard to catch up. Aaron couldn't believe how fast Caleb actually was. It seemed he'd never fully turned his speed on for the kids at practice, and it was impressive to Aaron every time he did it.

As they drove down the ice, the Boston defense worked to cut them off. Dimitri and Caleb had their give-and-go down, though, and the puck passed easily between them. Caleb drove deep, leaving Dimitri, the other wing, and the two D to set up. Caleb hard stopped and spun, looking for a pass. Before he got it off his stick, he was checked into the boards and ended up grappling for the puck with a Boston defenseman.

Caleb won the scuffle and sent the puck sailing around the boards. He'd barely gotten the black disc away before the D cross-checked him, causing Caleb to drop to the ice. The crowd erupted in boos and catcalls as the ref at the goal line whistled play to stop. Aaron had seen Caleb take hits before, but this one seemed particularly vengeful. He was thrilled that Caleb bounced right up as soon as he had space to do so. The last thing he needed was to get hurt again.

Boston called a time-out as their player got a two-minute penalty. Aaron watched as Caleb and the rest of his line came back to the bench. He didn't look into the stands, focusing on the coach instead. When the ref blew the whistle to line up for the face-off, Caleb, Dimitri, and their line mates took a seat as another line went out for the power play.

"Why they'd do that? Why not let them play?" Aaron looked to Grant, who he hoped knew more about the strategies of the game than he did.

"Most likely they want to keep the first line for the final

minute in case Boston pulls the goalie. The next two minutes will be okay, but it'll get dicey once the power play is over because Boston isn't going to let this go easily."

The penalty passed with no goals, but a lot of shots on net from the Rangers. As the penalty ended, there was just over a minute left. Caleb and Dimitri headed back out, and the home crowd went wild. Aaron was on his feet, as was most of The Garden. If New York held the score, they'd win. If Boston scored, it'd mean the risk of overtime, where anything could happen. The play was intense and, sure enough, as soon as the puck got into the Rangers' zone, the Boston goalie darted to the bench so a sixth attacker could take to the ice.

The way the players moved reminded Aaron of bees buzzing around—Boston looking for a score and New York looking to prevent it. With twenty-three seconds to go, Caleb, who was positioned in the slot, intercepted the puck, shrugged off the Boston defenseman who was nearest, and took off down the ice. The defensemen who'd been on Dimitri gave chase. Once Caleb was over the red line at center ice, he shot, and the puck sailed unobstructed into Boston's net.

The New York fans erupted into cheers as the Rangers players spilled off the bench and everyone rushed Caleb. He hadn't won the game—technically that goal happened earlier in the period—but he had all but sealed the win. It was possible in twenty seconds to get two goals and force overtime, but it was highly unlikely Boston would get even one.

When the final horn sounded the score was four to two. Aaron and Grant shared a high five while Caleb sent a warm smile to Aaron before he left the bench and headed for the locker room.

"Come on," Grant said. "I'll take you where you can wait for him while he does press and gets cleaned up."

They headed back the way they'd come, through the lounge where some of the people didn't even seem aware the game was over as they talked and ate. Aaron felt like questioning eyes were on him again as he passed through with Grant.

TWENTY-TWO

THE ACTIVITY around Aaron was dizzying. He'd been in a waiting area, deep inside Madison Square Garden, since Grant escorted him there after the game ended about twenty minutes ago. He'd dropped into a chair along the wall so he'd be out of the way in the packed room and hadn't moved in almost half an hour. The walls were lined with hockey and basketball action photos. There were stylishly upholstered couches and chairs along the perimeter, as well as a table set up with food and a bar with drinks. Lots of space was left open for people to mingle.

Even when he'd gone to Tyson's games, where he was always *just a friend*, there'd never been anything like this. Anaheim Stadium had deluxe seating, but Tyson had never put him there. Plus, Aaron had never waited for Tyson in a room like this. He usually had to meet him somewhere away from the ballfield for anything they did after a game.

Just like during the game, Aaron was sure everyone was looking at him and wondering why he was there. Thankfully, security didn't show up again. And no one said anything, but they didn't have to because Aaron's mind made up plenty of stories on its own. To add to his discomfort, there were celebrities present.

What the hell was he doing here?

On a large TV across the room, the press conference played and Aaron's heart soared at seeing Caleb next to the coach. He was in his black undershirt, and the suspenders that held up his pants were over his shoulders. His hair was a sweaty, rumpled mess. And he was totally adorable.

Caleb had played great, with two goals—including the one that clinched the game—and two assists. He'd had a hand in every goal the Rangers scored. It was like he hadn't been away for two months. Aaron had watched him have fun—there was no other description for it—for more than two hours. Even on the bench, he seemed animated and happy with his teammates.

The sound on the TV was down, and Aaron suddenly wished he could hear because Caleb was taking questions from the press. While they were probably only about his return and the team's chances at going all the way to the championship, he wanted to hear Caleb's voice. The sooner he finished, the sooner they'd be on their way from here.

Grant made his way through the crowd and squatted down next to the chair Aaron sat in. "Sorry this is taking a while. First game back and first playoff game make it a perfect storm of everyone wanting a moment with him."

"It's fine. He's got a job to do."

Grant smiled and nodded. "You doing okay here?"

Aaron shrugged. "It's kinda weird, but yeah." He leaned in so he could whisper. "Is that Taylor Kitsch over there? It looks like him, but—"

"Yeah. It's not the first time I've seen him here. I think I saw Matthew Perry earlier too."

"Oh my God, that was him. I wasn't sure. That's crazy."

"You get used to it." Grant leaned in a little bit more, so Aaron did as well. "The first game Caleb had me here with him, Justin Timberlake was in here. I'd come in to get Caleb's guests because they had a locker room visit, and there's Justin, looking all cool and incredibly handsome. I about died." They chuckled as Grant stole a look at the TV. "They're wrapping up, so I need to go to make sure he doesn't get hijacked by overzealous reporters."

Aaron watched the action on the screen. "How can you tell it's almost done?"

"The coach is clutching his papers. That's a sign he's had enough and is about to call it a night."

"That's kinda funny."

"It's an interesting quirk for sure." Grant stood. "I'll get Caleb to finish up as fast as possible. And feel free to have some food or something. You don't have to stay rooted to the chair." Grant clapped him on the shoulder, and Aaron smiled up at him.

Grant was stopped at the door to the waiting room by someone in a well-tailored suit. They talked briefly, and it looked like Grant had gestured in Aaron's direction, but that had to be wrong. He didn't know anyone here except Caleb and Grant.

To stop fixating on what was going on around him, Aaron decided to take Grant's suggestion and get some food. He extricated himself from the chair and went to the table, where it looked like a sports bar had exploded. Wings, sliders, and lots more covered the surface. He grabbed a plate, a couple of sliders, and a Coke.

Turning away from the bar, he almost ran right into the guy Grant had been talking to. Great, now he would be the guy who couldn't manage to get food without making a scene.

"Oh, excuse me."

"No problem. We avoided disaster. I just wanted to introduce myself. Phil Strauss." He extended a hand, and Aaron had to get his small plate perched on top of his plastic glass so he had a hand free. "I'm Caleb's agent. I figured I should meet the man who's caught Caleb's eye."

"Pleasure to meet you." Aaron had a bad feeling about this, but he couldn't put his finger on why. The guy had to be okay since Caleb seemed to surround himself with good people. Although he remembered when Caleb hung up on his agent too....

"Walk with me for a moment?"

"Uh. Sure." Was this when he'd be murdered in some dark corner of The Garden? It suddenly felt very horror-film.

"Don't worry. I'll have you back before Caleb's changed."

Aaron set the food down, untouched, but kept the soda because his throat had turned into a desert. He was at Phil's side as the agent guided them from the waiting room. Phil stayed quiet for a few moments, until they turned down a hall that had no one else in it.

"I understand that you and Caleb have known each other since high school."

"Longer, really." At least Aaron's voice worked despite the dryness. "I've been best friends with his sister since grade school, so he was always around." He took a drink.

"So you know he's played hockey most of his life."

Aaron nodded, keeping his expression neutral even while his annoyance grew. "Of course. I went to lot of his games back in the day, hanging out with Pam. I was there when he made his decision, after his last game playing for

Foster Grove's youth league, that his number was forever going to be twenty-eight because of Gordie Howe."

"Then you know that hockey *is* his thing," Phil said, crossing his arms. "He's easily got a good five, maybe ten years left in the league if he can stop breaking bones. So, I'm curious what the plan is for you two. Are you planning to move down here and spend the off-seasons in Foster Grove? Is this going to be more of a long-distance thing? Or is it something that was just a fling that's ending now that he's recovered?"

Who did this imperious jerk think he was? Aaron was furious and struggled to keep his anger in check. "We're figuring out what's next."

"Since my job is looking out for Caleb's interests, I wanted to know what your answer was. Caleb doesn't need any unnecessary distractions. In my view, if this is serious, the sooner you move down here, the better. Spouses and serious girlfriends or boyfriends all live around here. Or you can end it and Caleb does what's needed to forget about you. Whatever it is, it needs to happen soon so Caleb doesn't want to constantly go upstate. He's been back two days, and he's already said he's looking forward to a couple days off so he can go there."

Anger gave way to hurt. "This is really none of your business. I understand that you—"

"Aaron, there you are," Grant said, coming up from behind. "I was afraid Taylor Kitsch abducted you." He chuckled at his joke. "Phil, do you mind if I take him?"

"Not at all." Phil's intense glare made Aaron uncomfortable, but he met it head-on. He'd never see this man again anyway. "I think we're good here."

"Great." If Grant felt the tension between them, he didn't let on. He sounded as upbeat as always. Aaron was surprised when he took hold of his forearm and led him away. They were silent until they rounded a corner. Grant looked back before he said a word, and even then, he spoke softly. "What did Phil say? You look like you're about to explode. I mean, I don't know you all that well, but—"

"He was... making his concerns known."

Grant sighed. "Sorry. I shouldn't have left you two alone. I should've just introduced you and made sure he left with me. Sometimes he can be a little gruff."

"That's one way to put it."

They passed the waiting room Aaron had been in. Where were they going?

"Caleb will be ready to go in just a few minutes—and believe me, he's ready to get out of here." Grant opened a door and gestured for Aaron to enter. "You'll be out of the crowd here, and Phil shouldn't look for you here either. If anyone asks, just tell them I put you here."

This room was nicer than the room he'd been waiting in. It didn't have the catering, but there were more places to sit. One wall was taken up with a long mirror and a counter with chairs in front. Aaron assumed it must be a dressing room used when concerts played here.

"I don't want to get you in trouble." Aaron looked to Grant. "I can deal with Phil."

"Don't worry about it." Grant smiled, and Aaron tried to relax. "I know I shouldn't—" He stopped short, looking conflicted. "Let me just get Caleb so you guys can be on your way."

Grant turned to go, but Aaron caught him by the arm. "What? Tell me."

"I shouldn't have opened my mouth, but... here it is—I think he really wants to make it work with you. He hasn't said anything directly about it, but I've never seen him as happy as when he talks about you. He was practically jumping up and down when you agreed to come for the weekend. I heard some of what Phil said. Don't let him sway your decisions."

Aaron gave a weak smile. "Thanks."

Except Phil was right. He was a distraction to Caleb and that was the last thing he wanted to be. He'd seen how happy Caleb was tonight—on the ice, with his teammates. He couldn't stand in the way of that.

Grant's phone chirped, and he smiled as he checked the screen and typed a quick message. "Caleb's on his way. I hope you guys have a good day tomorrow. I promise I'll have him back from the radio gig by ten. Unless you want to come hang out?"

Aaron quickly shook his head. "No, thanks. If I'm there, it may lead to more questions about us."

"Fair enough."

Before Grant could say more, Caleb entered, and Aaron was momentarily breathless at how handsome he looked in his game-day attire. The dark blue suit had been expertly tailored to accentuate his muscular frame. The sky-blue dress shirt set off his blue eyes perfectly. The red tie was the perfect accent, given New York's colors. Since Aaron had arrived after Caleb was already in the locker room, it was his first time to see this dressed-up side of Caleb in person.

"It's so good to see you." Caleb went right up to Aaron, wrapped him in a light embrace, and kissed him. It was brief, and the step back made Aaron's body ache for more. It had only been a few days, but he hadn't realized how much he missed him.

"Great game. You were incredible out there." Aaron stuck to the game since he wasn't sure what else to say.

"Thanks. I loved seeing you behind the bench. I'd love to have you there all the time."

Aaron struggled with what to say next because so many thoughts vied to get out. He shouldn't be nervous around Caleb, but this was getting insane.

A knock at the ajar door made it so he didn't have to speak.

"There you are! Get in here." Grant stepped to the side as Caleb pulled in one of his fellow players. The handsome man's dark hair was slicked back, and he wore a well-tailored suit similar to Caleb's. "Aaron, this is my best friend, Dimitri."

Dimitri smiled rakishly and extended a hand. Aaron hesitated for only a moment before his manners kicked in. He hadn't expected to meet any of Caleb's teammates, at least not yet. "Good to finally meet you," Dimitri said. "I thought we could go grab a late dinner and hang out for a while."

"I'm up for that if Aaron is." Caleb raised his eyebrows and looked expectantly at Aaron.

"Sure." Aaron couldn't say no to Caleb's silent request. The weekend was supposed to show Aaron all about New York life, and time with one of Caleb's closest friends should be part of it.

"I'll bring the car to the loading dock so you can get out without too much fuss." Grant was almost out the door before he stopped and turned back to them. "Do you need reservations anywhere?"

"I got this." Dimitri looked proud of himself. "I'd hoped Aaron would say yes, so I rang up one of my favorite places on the Lower East Side, where we should be out of the postgame fray." Dimitri clapped Caleb on the back before saying his goodbyes. "I'll meet you guys there."

"Give me five minutes, and I should have the car in place. I'll text you when I'm there." Grant headed out too.

"I'm so glad you're here," Caleb said, wrapping Aaron in a tight embrace. "Are you having a good time so far?"

"I guess." Aaron's entire body seemed to shrug. "The game was amazing. Watching you in person is so much better than on TV. All of this back here"—Aaron gestured around—"it's a little much. I wish I'd gone back to your place to wait."

Caleb deflated a little, and Aaron wished he'd kept his mouth shut. "I hadn't considered what all this would be like with no one to hang out with."

"It's okay. You had a job to do."

"Let's relax and get some dinner." Caleb took his hand. "That should let us ease into a day that will be mostly all about us."

"Let's do it," Aaron said, managing to sound upbeat.

"Let's go to where Grant's bringing the car, so we'll be ready as soon as it's there." Caleb led them to the loading dock so they'd be ready to go.

TWENTY-THREE

AARON GAZED out of the wall of windows of Caleb's sixth-floor loft. The view of the Hudson River was gorgeous on the clear spring night. He'd gravitated to the windows when they'd come in from dinner with Dimitri a few minutes ago. Aaron had a good time hearing all the stories Dimitri shared. Dimitri knew Caleb at this point in his life far better than Aaron did.

"Hey. You look really good there." Caleb, returning from the kitchen with two bottles of water, came over and stood next to him. "Grant texted that he's got us a brunch reservation at eleven thirty at a place in Chelsea he says we'll love. We can head there as soon as I'm back from the radio thing. You ready for the grand tour?"

Aaron liked Grant. He seemed genuinely nice and took good care of Caleb, making sure he met all of his commitments.

And Caleb had a lot of professional obligations. What Phil had said earlier continued to gnaw at him. The truth was, Aaron *was* a distraction. There were so many things that Caleb should be doing to stay on track for the playoffs and for his contract negotiations. If he was to have a boyfriend, it should be someone who understood how to navigate it all, not an outsider with no experience in the spotlight. And not someone who'd had a mess of a relationship with a baseball player. How was he supposed to make it work with Caleb, whose celebrity was orders of magnitude greater than Tyson's?

Aaron sighed, feeling overwhelmed by the night. "I was thinking I should head back. You can rest up tomorrow and be ready to dominate on Sunday afternoon, and I can get back and prepare for class next week."

"What?" Caleb sounded disappointed, as Aaron expected.

"We're fooling ourselves to think I could possibly belong here, doing this." He tried to look at Caleb but quickly turned back toward the river view. "I'm glad we spent more time together, but you've got enough to do without making sure I'm happy. You've done it subtly ever since I got here, when you were looking at me in the stands and while we've been together after the game. You steal these looks at me to make sure I'm okay. You need to be focused on the game, on the Stanley Cup, on your career. Not if everything's all right with your boyfriend who's out of his depth."

Caleb turned Aaron to him. "Sure, I'm checking on you, but it's because I care about you and you're visiting a place you've hardly been to before. Where's this coming from?"

"Caleb. Think about it. You've worked so hard to get where you are. You love what you do—anyone could see that when you played tonight. And the truth is that I love what I do. I love teaching, and I still feel like I'm getting my life back together. You don't need to deal with my baggage."

"Aaron—"

"Please let me get this out. It's hard enough already." Aaron looked Caleb in the eye and prayed he had enough courage to finish. "I don't want you to wonder why you stuck it out with me when you could've had anyone. I refuse to be the one to hold you back or the one you regret later. I can't stand the thought of messing up the life of someone I care so much about simply because I'm—"

"I love you, Aaron Price!" Caleb blurted out as he grabbed hold of Aaron and brought him in for a kiss, which nearly unhinged him because it was the most passionate kiss he'd ever received. It also pissed him off because that kiss did nothing to help get his point across. Aaron's body didn't listen to his brain. It took over, kissing Caleb back. They continued until Aaron released a long, low moan of pleasure.

Aaron moved away from Caleb, out of reach. "It's not fair that you can kiss like that. How am I supposed to—?" Aaron had no idea what to say next.

"Supposed to what? Tell me why you think we can't work? I don't want to hear it."

"I don't know how to do this," Aaron said as he tried to figure out what to do with himself. If he sat, Caleb could easily trap him and plant another kiss on him. But he couldn't stay where he was because it was too close. He decided to stand on the other side of the couch to put distance between them.

"Why's it so important to figure that out now?" Caleb pushed on, moving around the furniture, toward Aaron. "Let's decide to be a couple and go from there. Isn't what's most important is that we are in love?"

There was *love* again. Aaron's heart and soul wanted to say it back, but practicality won out. "You know as well as I do that it takes work to make a relationship successful. It's more than a few words. It's constant attention."

"Athletes—hockey players—make this work all the time. Not everyone's like that asshole you were with in LA." Frustration crept into Caleb's voice as he once again reached for Aaron's hand. Aaron moved his hand away but didn't step back. "The goalie in Las Vegas married the woman he'd dated since he was fifteen. They've got kids and she owns a business. They make it work. Nashville's captain married a country music star. I've talked to him a time or two about the challenges of their schedule, but they've been married nearly a decade. Many of my teammates are in relationships. They're not all like Dimitri. Come to Sunday's game, and you can meet them and see for yourself."

Caleb could teach a course in persuasion. He said the right things in the right way, which picked at Aaron's facade of resistance.

"Please, Aaron. I can't make things right if you don't tell me what you're thinking." Caleb didn't try to touch Aaron.

"Where do I start? I was raised that relationships should be on equal ground, and there's so much between us that wouldn't be. The money. The fame. The expectations. That thing with the picture was just a sample, I'm sure. It's all my kids wanted to talk about last week. It's not a fair distraction for them to see their teacher like that."

"But that was a surprise to us both. If we're a couple, and everyone knows that, seeing pictures won't be a distraction." Caleb smiled, as if he enjoyed the thoughts he had. "If you're introduced as my boyfriend, it'll become no big deal."

"Can you imagine me out with you at an event or something?" He looked at Caleb, who continued with the easy smile while Aaron thought of terrifying scenarios. "I wouldn't know what to talk about."

"You'd do fine. Trust me, it's really no different than the carnival. Conversations just get randomly started. And you're a smart man. You teach. That's an important career in itself. Plus, you'd be with me. And you'd be around the team. Dimitri already likes you, and I know the others will too. The wives, girlfriends, and boyfriends band together to take care of one another."

Aaron raised an eyebrow as their standoff continued. They were close enough to do any number of things to each other—things Aaron wanted but couldn't allow himself to have.

"Yes, there are other boyfriends," Caleb said. "One of our defensemen has a long-term boyfriend, and D sometimes brings guys too."

Aaron had no words. He hadn't expected Caleb to put up such a strong argument. Yet he felt like he was back in high school and looking at the athletes from the outside, as one of the brainy guys no one really wanted to be around. It was a stupid feeling that he couldn't shake because Tyson had played on that late in their relationship as a way to control him.

Caleb didn't let up. "Do you realize how much you mean to me? How much you've shown me over the past couple of weeks about what I want in my life? I didn't realize what I was missing. We've always had this connection—even back in high school it was easy to be around you, though you were, like, a million times smarter than I was. You never made me feel less than you."

"You really only had issues in math, you know," Aaron said quietly.

"Still. You could've given me shit or been a condescending dick during our tutoring sessions. I know how the smart students felt about us jocks."

Aaron wanted so badly to kiss Caleb, but that wouldn't help finish this. He was being so earnest.

"We could end up hurting each other little by little, until there's nothing left. Maybe we need one of those pacts." Aaron already dreaded the words. "You know, if we're not married by the time you retire, then we get together. Until then, it's not really practical."

Caleb's head dropped in disappointment. Aaron wasn't happy he'd zapped him like that, but there wasn't a choice.

"I fucking hate practical." Caleb looked back to Aaron, who saw the hurt in his eyes. "We could be great right now and forever. Tell me, what do I need to do to prove that to you?"

Aaron shook his head as he fought to control his emotions. The sadness in Caleb's eyes and his pained voice punched him in the gut repeatedly. "I'll have to trust that time will bring us back together if it's supposed to be."

"What if that's not what I want?"

Aaron shook. He was losing his internal battle. "It's not what I want either, but I think it has to be, for both of our sakes." He brought Caleb's hand to his mouth and planted a kiss on the knuckles. "I think I should go before we do something we'll regret."

"Aaron, no...." Caleb's voice cracked, and it stabbed at Aaron.

"Please, Caleb."

Caleb released Aaron's hand. "I'm going to keep looking for something that will persuade you that this—us—can work."

Aaron headed for the door and picked up his bag, which he'd never unpacked.

"I meant what I said—I love you, Aaron."

Aaron slipped out the door with those words echoing in his head. He knew he'd made the right choice, but that didn't change the ache in his heart.

TWENTY-FOUR

"New York goal to number twenty-eight, Caleb Carter. Assisted by number fifty-seven, Dimitri Stanislov, at fifteen thirty-three in the third period."

The Boston crowd booed the announcement. So far, game three in the Rangers-Bruins series was on New York's side with the clock running out.

Caleb was back on the bench, alongside Dimitri, as the announcement was made. It was the third time they'd been called out during the game, much to the annoyance of the home crowd. It was Caleb's first goal of the night. He'd picked up assists on two of Dimitri's in the second.

"We're on fire tonight." Dimitri clapped Caleb on the back. "Wish we were playing this one for the home crowd."

"Yeah. It feels great." Caleb smiled and picked up his water bottle from the ledge in front of him. Squirting water into his mouth, he wished he could feel more excited. His game was on autopilot, and thankfully, his instincts had him playing at the high level the team needed.

The skating—for practice and the games—was all that had kept him together since Aaron had left him four days before. Somehow, he'd made it through Sunday's game without getting into what had happened. Even Grant and Dimitri hadn't pressed him, allowing him to simply say Aaron had gone home.

While being on the ice felt good, Foster Grove was where he ached to be, to get another chance with Aaron. He'd hoped his proclamation that he loved Aaron would give them time to sort out what a relationship could be. Aaron had devastated him by walking out despite the fact that Caleb was sure Aaron felt the same way he did. He wished he could go to LA and find the guy who had hurt him so much.

Dimitri pushed against his shoulder and snapped him back to reality. "You gonna scoot?"

"Sorry." Caleb slid down the bench since they were getting closer to another shift.

"Where'd you go?"

Caleb didn't want to get into what he was really thinking about, so he defaulted back to something to do with the game. Talking strategy was a good choice. "Just thinking about that last goal. Dissecting it so maybe we can do it again. We totally confused their defense with our zigzag pattern."

Dimitri looked at him for a moment as if that wasn't what he expected to hear.

"What if we mix it up a bit?" Caleb suggested.

Thankfully, Dimitri went along with it and grabbed one of the whiteboards from behind them. He drew a variation on what they'd done their last time out. "What do you think?"

Caleb studied the board for a moment. "Let's do it." He was excited for the on-the-fly strategy making.

"Looks good, guys," Coach chimed in, standing over them.

The trio went back out with less than a minute on the clock. Dimitri's last-second shot had to be reviewed because the horn sounded. Ultimately, the goal was denied because the puck didn't fully cross the goal line before the clock ran out. But they had a new play to work on because the pattern they'd discussed worked, and if they refined it, they could try it again for game four. New York won four to three, and if they beat Boston in the next meeting, they'd sweep the series.

Dimitri and Caleb both got "Three Stars of the Night" honors, alongside the Boston goalie, who kept it from being more of a blowout. Caleb was proud to earn that title anytime he could, and even more so on someone else's ice. It was bittersweet tonight, though. He wondered if Aaron watched the game. Despite having played well, Caleb knew it would've just added to Aaron's argument that they didn't belong together.

"I was that close to a hat trick," Dimitri grumbled, holding up his thumb and forefinger with little space between them.

"Sorry, man. We still rocked that game," Caleb said as they headed to the visitors' locker room.

"Yes, we did!" That was all it took for Dimitri to snap out of his no-hat-trick funk.

Once everyone gathered inside, Coach addressed the team from the middle of the room. "Well done tonight, guys. Now we just have to keep our focus. Thursday's game will send a message about how serious we are this postseason. Get some rest tonight. We'll skate tomorrow at two."

As Coach left, the team got back to celebrating their third win in a row. Caleb was quiet. Soon enough, they'd be back at the hotel and he could try to get to sleep—luckily, he'd been exhausted enough from the games and practices that his mind had no choice but to shut down for rest.

A phone chirp stopped him while he stood in front of his locker. He took it off the shelf, hoping beyond hope he'd see Aaron's name on the screen. They hadn't spoken since he'd walked out.

Instead, Caleb found a text from Pam. *Way to go, little bro. Second star of the game on another team's ice. You looked great out there.*

He smiled. Pam was always a fan; so were his parents, but they were still on their trip. They'd been keeping up and sending him emails, which always ended with them telling him to be careful.

He typed back. *Thanks! It was fun. And you should get to bed, you've got school tomorrow.* He added a winky face.

As he sent it, he stared at the word *fun*. It was fun, and it was wrong that it was fun. Or was it? He loved hockey. He also loved Aaron. Aaron liked hockey. Did Aaron love Caleb? He hadn't said it even though Caleb said it twice. There was some weird word problem in all this. "If Caleb loves Aaron and hockey, and Aaron...."

"Everything okay?" Dimitri interrupted his math problem.

"Uh. Yeah." Caleb put the phone back on the locker shelf. "Pam sent congratulations."

"You and I both know that's not what you're thinking about."

Dimitri wasn't going to keep to himself much longer. Caleb met his gaze for just a moment longer but didn't say anything. He simply sighed.

"I gotta go do the press," Caleb said and turned for the door as Dimitri nodded in acknowledgment.

By the time he got to the shower, most of the team was done and dressing. As time clicked by, it seemed like the game had occurred in the distant past. His mind returned to the Aaron situation. Pam hadn't said anything about Aaron, and yet she had to know at least the basics of what happened. Was her silence good or bad? He wanted to ask her how Aaron was doing, but that seemed intrusive. While she was his sister, she was also Aaron's best friend, and Caleb didn't want to put her in a position to violate any secrets.

Once he was back in the suit he'd arrived in, he went into the room where he could wait comfortably since the bus hadn't arrived yet. He dropped into a chair, away from the others in the room, and closed his eyes. He felt like he was stuck watching a movie on repeat as scenes of Aaron and him played in his mind—a mix of good times and the horrible finality of Friday night. Caleb had wanted the New York weekend to solidify the start of something, not the end.

A few minutes later, he was forced to open his eyes because someone kicked his feet. It was no surprise that it was Dimitri.

"Did you eat?"

Caleb shook his head. "Not yet."

Dimitri grunted. "I thought so. I grabbed your usual turkey and some of that nasty blue Powerade you like." He handed it over, his expression one of concern.

"Thanks."

"The bus is here." Dimitri was being unusually quiet, given their game win. Caleb knew he would forgo celebrating to look after him. "We've got a few minutes if you want to eat here, or we can board."

"Let's get on the bus." Caleb stood and gave Dimitri's shoulder a quick squeeze.

Dimitri nodded, and they headed for the exit, a couple of their teammates in front of them.

Outside, there were a few people waiting. It was a shared entrance, but given it was Boston's arena, most of the crowd wore the home team's apparel.

"Mr. Carter?"

They both stopped, and Caleb turned to where a teenager stood off by himself, wearing a Boston sweatshirt. Caleb wasn't often stopped by people in the opposing team's gear, so the callout confused him. The guy didn't look like he was old enough to be out of high school.

"Yes? Hi." Caleb sounded as chipper as he could. Even though he felt like crap, he wasn't going to be rude to anyone. He walked to where the young man waited behind the barriers that kept the walkway out of the arena clear.

"Um. Hi. Um." The boy's eyes darted around as if he was nervous. "I was wondering if you'd sign this. I know you're not commenting on it... but... well. It was...."

Caleb looked at the picture of the kiss he'd shared with Aaron. It was a little fuzzy and didn't take up the entire paper it was on. Dimitri put his hand on Caleb's shoulder, and that almost unleashed his emotions. It was more comfort than he deserved because he'd blown it with Aaron.

"I'm sorry. I didn't mean...." The boy started to withdraw the paper when Caleb did nothing but stare at it. "I shouldn't have."

"It's okay." Caleb's voice came out a bit strangled, so he cleared his throat. He handed his food to Dimitri before taking the picture from the boy "Of course I'll sign it. Do you have a pen?"

"Sure." The boy brightened, and that helped Caleb regain his composure. He handed over a black Sharpie. "It was cool to see this picture. I'm... I'm gay." The boy dropped his voice to a whisper. "And I play. I know you are, and he is too." He gestured at Dimitri. "But I don't tell anyone. My team is always talking crap and saying... well, you know. But seeing a picture of you kissing this guy, it means it's possible to play and have a boyfriend. It was just.... Sorry, I'm totally babbling."

Caleb signed his name and handed the paper and the pen back. He didn't correct the young man that he and Aaron weren't together. "Can you be out to anyone?"

More of Caleb's teammates passed them as they talked, but they didn't stop.

"My parents know and they're cool, and now you two. I can't do it at school with my friends or the team. I see how the few out guys at school are treated—not bullied, exactly, but shunned, made fun of. I don't think I can do that."

"Five minutes, guys." One of the equipment managers gave them a time check as more of the team left the arena.

Caleb thought fast, not really sure he was about to suggest the right thing. "Sometimes it just takes one person to stand up and be a leader to make change. How about I come talk to your team sometime? Or maybe your school? I could probably talk someone from the Bruins into joining me so it wouldn't be some random New York player showing up. Maybe we can make it better together."

"You'd do that?" The boy was clearly surprised.

"I'd be honored to." Caleb got his wallet from his pants pocket and pulled out a card. "Email my assistant. I'll tell him we talked and what needs to be done. He'll help get it coordinated."

"Wow. Thanks." He took the card, turning it over in his hand.

"Thank you. It's good to meet you...."

"I'm David Eisenberg."

Caleb extended his fist, which David met. Dimitri and David exchanged a fist bump too. "We've got to get going. But we'll be talking."

"Thanks, Mr. Carter."

"It's Caleb. You take care, okay?"

"Yes, sir."

Caleb turned and waved after they were a few steps away, and David gave an enthusiastic wave back.

On the bus, Caleb and Dimitri took their usual seats, midway back on the right, with Caleb at the window. He held his food but leaned his head against the glass and closed his eyes. He was happy he could maybe help David and spread the word on tolerance and equality. What kept running through his mind, though, was that Aaron would've loved that exchange.

Dimitri squeezed Caleb's arm. "I'll listen whenever you're ready."

It was as if Dimitri read Caleb's mind.

Caleb nodded but didn't move. He worked to keep his emotions in check, not so much for Dimitri, but for the rest of the team. The fact that he'd played so well and yet ached this much for Aaron spoke volumes to him about how important he had become.

"We'll get a couple beers from room service, and then I'll...." Caleb said, looking at Dimitri, who simply gave a single nod.

TWENTY-FIVE

AARON SAT ALONE in his classroom. The final bell of the day had rung a couple of minutes ago and the students cleared out quickly. Aaron had nothing planned after school, so he was trying to focus on grading some papers.

He would watch hockey tonight—that much was certain. The Rangers looked good to close out their series with Boston, and he wasn't going to miss the chance to see Caleb, who was playing great. As much as it hurt, it meant Aaron had made the right choice because Caleb had rarely looked better on the ice.

A knock at the classroom door pulled Aaron from his thoughts. "Come in."

"Hi, Mr. Price. I forgot my action figures."

"No problem, Charlie. Come on in." Aaron chuckled. Some things never changed. He had brought action figures to elementary school, and kids still did it. Aaron busied himself by organizing the papers that needed his attention.

Charlie quickly got what he needed from his desk and stuffed the handful of figures into his bag. He paused coming back up the aisle. "You okay, Mr. Price?"

Aaron stopped, two clipped stacks of paper in his hand, and looked at Charlie. "Yes. Of course. Why?"

Charlie shrugged. "You don't smile much anymore."

Crap. He'd been working so hard to keep his sadness away from the kids. So much for that. Smiles would have to be on display starting tomorrow for sure.

Aaron forced his lips to curve upward in the approximation of a smile, hoping that he wasn't grimacing. "Everything's fine. I'm just tired since I'm helping out one of the hockey coaches."

"Oh, okay." Charlie perked up hearing he was okay. He quickly headed for the door, but stopped just short, turning back to Aaron. "If my mom thinks I'm tired, she makes me take a nap. Maybe you should do that."

"I just might," Aaron said, complete with a genuine smile. Charlie touched him with his concern and the remedy.

"See you tomorrow, Mr. Price." Charlie took off running. Aaron knew he should stop him from running in the hallway, but he probably had a parent waiting.

"He's right, you know." It was Pam, leaning against the doorframe. "I haven't seen a smile in almost a week, and you're dragging around like you've lost your best friend."

"That, thankfully, I've still got." Aaron stuffed the papers into his bag, along with the other things he'd need for the evening.

"You want to come over, make some popcorn and maybe something chocolatey?"

"You gonna watch the game?" He walked toward her, slinging his bag over his shoulder.

"I wasn't going to put you through that. We can watch something else. Whatever you want."

"Actually"—he sounded ashamed to admit this, even to his own ears—"I'd like to watch the game. It's... I haven't been able to *not* watch. I've tried, and the TV ends up on anyway. It'll be good to watch with someone else."

"The game it is, then."

Aaron didn't miss the concern in her voice.

"Have you talked to him?"

She nodded as they walked down the empty school hallway. "Just once, before he went up to Boston. But not about you. I haven't pressed him, just like I haven't pushed to get you to talk. Other than that, we trade texts about the games."

"He's doing okay?"

She shrugged. "I think he's going through the motions to do what he needs to do. He's arranging to have the youth team come down for one of the round two home games. He's trying to make it so they can skate on the ice at The Garden too."

"They'll love that, even if it's just the game." Just another aspect of Caleb for Aaron to love. Why did his mind have to insert that word—*love*? It was accurate, though. Caleb had gone out of his way to help the kids in practice. Making it so they can attend a playoff game was just an extension of that.

In the parking lot, they took a moment before they went their cars. "See you before the first face-off?"

"Yeah. I'll be there a little before seven thirty."

"Perfect."

Aaron got in his car, thankful he wasn't going to be home watching the game solo tonight. Maybe he'd pull out of his rut this weekend. The youth team played Saturday and Sunday, and he could go watch. He enjoyed working with them, and while it'd be a reminder of Caleb, being around the other parents and the kids would probably be good for him.

On the way home, his mind replayed all the arguments he had for not being with Caleb. As much as he knew Caleb wasn't—and could never be—Tyson, he kept focusing on how bad his last relationship was. He'd done research and looked up the hockey players Caleb mentioned and found many others who seemingly had thriving marriages.

It was harder to deny there was a hole in his life that seemed to grow larger the more he didn't see, or at least talk to, Caleb.

It was silly. It wasn't like they'd spent every moment of every day together when Caleb was in town. But when he'd been there, they usually saw each other for at least part of every day.

At home, Aaron headed straight for the bedroom to get out of his school clothes. His phone chirped as he emptied his pockets. The lock screen showed it was a text from Grant, which was odd. He hadn't heard from Grant since his New York trip. The text was simple: *Wanted to make sure you saw this.* There was a Facebook URL.

Aaron's finger hovered over the URL. Grant was a good guy; there was no way he'd send something better left unseen. Aaron clicked to a public Facebook post from a teenager named David Eisenberg. Aaron didn't know where to look first because he was stunned by what was on screen. The photo showed David holding up the picture of Aaron and Caleb, with Caleb's autograph beneath it. In the text, Aaron saw Caleb and Dimitri were tagged.

Thanks to Caleb Carter and Dimitri Stanislov for spending a few minutes talking to me after last night's

Rangers/Bruins game. Caleb, you stopped even though you had food in your hand and were on the way to your bus. You even ignored that I had a Boston shirt on (sorry about that). You autographed this picture and mentioned that it only takes one person to step up and be a leader to make a change. That starts by saying right here, to everyone, that I'm gay. Thanks for helping me to see that it's okay for me to say that.

David's Facebook page showed that he went to a Boston high school, and there were pictures of him in hockey gear too. The comments on his post were overwhelmingly positive. Many congratulated him for *finally* coming out and said how cool it was that he'd met Caleb and Dimitri. There were a few nasty comments, and those were met head-on by David's friends and even David himself, who invited some of them to try to say those words to his face. Still others simply offered thanks for sharing his story.

One of the early comments was from Caleb—at the end of the post were his initials, which meant it wasn't Grant posting.

Congratulations on taking this step. I'm proud of you, and so is Dimitri. We've both got your back. We look forward to coming up to see you and your team. And you can still wear that Boston sweatshirt. :) ^CC

Farther down, another post caught his eye, this one from the Bruins' official team page.

We've got your back too, David. Caleb told us your story, and we look forward to working with him to spread the You Can Play message at your school. Stay strong and always remember you've got a lot of people on your team. And we'll understand if you start wearing a Rangers shirt—but only if it's one sporting Caleb's number.

Aaron set the phone on the dresser. He wasn't sure how

to process this. Caleb had always been a good guy, but this seemed above and beyond even for him. Aaron wished he could just pick up the phone and call Caleb to talk more about his random meeting with the teen hockey player. Calling, however, probably wouldn't be good for either one of them.

"I really fucked up," he said to the empty room. Maybe he should take the advice Caleb gave David and stand up for the change he wanted.

Would Caleb take him back if he asked? It was branded on Aaron's heart that Caleb had said that he loved Aaron. Twice. And Aaron hadn't reciprocated. He'd almost said it, but couldn't. Was Caleb even missing him?

Was the ball even in Aaron's court—or more aptly, was the puck in his zone? All of the reasons why a relationship wouldn't work had come from Aaron, while Caleb remained the optimist and actively shot them down. The puck was likely on Aaron's stick to make the next play. He could either ice it out of play or pass it to Caleb with some sign that they should continue.

Sure, there were ways it could work. Caleb had pointed those out. The trip wasn't bad by car. There was a train. Hell, Aaron knew people who commuted from southern New Jersey or Philly for work in NYC, and that could be a couple hours each way, every day. And it wasn't just hockey players who had to travel—many people did that and had good relationships. Aaron's arguments were stupid. Caleb was a good man, and Aaron had walked away.

Aaron shuddered, just as he'd done when he'd returned home from New York early Saturday morning. Realizations slammed into him, pushing his emotional buttons.

He grabbed the phone and sent a text to Pam. *Thanks for the invite. I'm gonna take a rain check. I need to think.*

He sent it and powered the phone off. He didn't want to be persuaded to come over or see anything else about Caleb. It was time to decide what to do about the man he was in love with.

TWENTY-SIX

CALEB WAS EXHAUSTED YET ELATED as Grant drove them into Foster Grove from the Albany airport on Friday afternoon. After sweeping Boston the night before, there were a few days before the second round of playoffs could begin—thankfully, a couple of matchups were headed into at least five games. He had to rejoin the team Monday for the morning skate, but he could take the weekend off and not impact his teammates.

He'd been awake most of the night worrying about his plan. Despite the fact that he knew in his heart it was perfect, he might still get shut down. If he was, Caleb resolved to let Aaron go. He had to make the last attempt, though, because he didn't want to be stuck with a *what-if* years from now.

Grant had driven up to Albany in Caleb's SUV not only to pick up his boss, but to bring him luggage for the weekend in the hopes that the trip was a success. If it was, Grant would rent a car to return to NYC, and if not, they'd go back together. The first stop was his parents' house to make a quick change of clothes so he'd be in something different than one of his game-day suits. He picked something similar to their dinner at FG Plate—a sweater-and-jeans combo.

Leaving Grant at his parents', he sped to the elementary school parking lot and arrived with a few minutes to go before the final bell. Violating school rules, he didn't check in at the main office and instead headed directly for Aaron's classroom.

"Caleb?"

He stopped as he heard Pam's confused voice behind him. She was coming out of the staff lounge, carrying a stack of folders clutched to her chest.

"What are you doing here?"

"Going for it." He grinned at her and turned back to continue his mission.

Her shoes clicked on the tile floor, following him.

The door to Aaron's classroom was open, and Caleb stood quietly, watching as the class read from a book he couldn't see the title of. A different student read each page, and Aaron offered word corrections if they pronounced something wrong. Aaron looked tired but still seemed vibrant in front of the class.

Pam put her hand on Caleb's shoulder as she stood behind him.

As the reading continued, one of the boys looked over and saw him in the doorway. Initially, the student went back to his book, but he kept looking over at Caleb every few seconds, until he finally raised his hand. Caleb wasn't looking to interrupt, but his quiet watching was about to be discovered.

"Yes, Charlie?" Aaron asked before the next student started to read.

"I think Mr. Carter is here to see you." Charlie pointed

at the door.

"I don't—" Aaron turned to face the door and his mouth dropped open.

Caleb couldn't tell what Aaron was thinking as he saw a mix of emotions play across his handsome features. Caleb's face heated as all eyes in the room turned to him. He had to do something. Standing there, gawking at Aaron, wasn't going to accomplish anything.

"Sorry to interrupt." Caleb stepped into the classroom and addressed the students. "I needed to see Mr. Price, and I got here a little early."

"Is everything all right?" Aaron sounded—and looked—concerned and confused.

Caleb stopped to consider and cocked his head. He met Aaron's gaze. "Well, I'm not sure yet."

Aaron swallowed hard, and Caleb wondered if Aaron's mouth was as dry as his was. He hadn't planned to say anything in front of the kids. They were young, after all, and he didn't want to make a fuss. The silence stretched on as Caleb didn't quite know how to continue.

"Are you going to help Mr. Price not be sad?" Charlie asked.

"Charlie, that's not—"

"I hope so."

Pam stepped around Caleb into the room. "Why don't you two go, and I'll finish up the last few minutes with the students?"

Caleb smiled quickly at his sister before fixing his eyes on Aaron and extending his hand. Aaron looked to his desk, the papers, and the messenger bag on the back of the chair.

"We'll come back for whatever you need. I promise."

Aaron nodded and took his outstretched hand. There

were some good-natured giggles from some of the students, and Caleb couldn't help but grin.

"This is quite a surprise," Aaron said once they were in the hall and headed toward the door. "How are you even here?"

"Sweeping the series means a weekend off." Caleb grinned and thought it was a good sign that Aaron hadn't pulled his hand away.

"I'm sorry about—"

"Don't say it. You don't have to apologize for what you said or how you felt. It's important we communicate to prevent even more problems."

They made their way outside to the school parking lot. They got to his car, and Caleb opened the passenger door for Aaron. He'd never done that before. Maybe it was to make sure Aaron didn't try and run away.

Aaron got in and was facing the driver's door when Caleb joined him. Without any indication where they were headed, Caleb started the car and pulled out of the lot. He'd considered a lot about how to do this and was still second-guessing himself.

"So, I need your opinion, which is one of the reasons I'm here. Can you get the... the thing out of the glove box?"

"The thing?"

Caleb saw Aaron's perplexed look from the corner of his eye. "I can't remember what the stupid thing's called right now. It's the only thing in there."

Aaron opened the compartment and pulled out the contents. "Paint colors? You want to talk about paint colors?" He sounded as confused as he looked, which was adorable.

"Did you know there are a couple dozen variations on white? It's insane," he said, turning toward downtown. "But

I'm curious what you consider white. I mean, is it as simple as what's labeled white? Or is it Frost or something like Silky White or Polar Bear. It's important to get it right."

It was good that Aaron's gaze seemed to go only between the fan deck of paint chips and Caleb. He'd picked a weird route to get them where they were going, and so far, Aaron hadn't seemed to notice.

"You realize you've completely lost me. Why are you asking me?"

"Because your opinion matters." Caleb pulled into the driveway of their destination. "It's your vision."

Aaron looked out the windshield and then out the passenger window. Caleb was sure Aaron would notice the large Sold sign in the front yard.

"What did you do?" Aaron's hand covered his mouth. As Caleb put the SUV into park, he noticed an almost imperceptible shudder from Aaron in the passenger seat.

He hustled out of the car and around to open Aaron's door. He couldn't control his happiness and thought his smile might be permanently etched on his face. "I need a place here, in Foster Grove, and I'm hoping you'll join me and make this *our* home."

"Oh my God. Caleb. Seriously?" His voice cracked, full of emotion.

Tears crept out of Aaron's eyes. He didn't sound angry. Caleb hoped he wasn't making a mess. He knew this could go very wrong and only highlight Aaron's arguments.

"It's one hundred percent ours." Caleb took Aaron's hand and led him to the front porch. "Now, about the paint color. I had them drop off some samples that we can put it on the trim to see how it looks."

The paints and a few brushes were right where Grant had said they'd be. He'd really pulled off some miracles in the past three days, and Caleb was going to give him a giant bonus.

"Having looked at the book thingy, I think regular white looks really good." Caleb reached down and grabbed the white, shook it as directed, and opened the container. He laid on a couple strokes of paint to the trim around the front door.

"What are you doing?" Aaron stood on the porch, still shaking.

"Trying to get you to pick a color." Caleb gave him a shy smile.

"You bought a house." Aaron's voice cracked as he looked around. "That's... I don't have words."

"Some might say *crazy*." Caleb set the paint down carefully and took Aaron's hands in his. "But I wanted to show you how serious I am about us. I want my life to be in Foster Grove, with you... if you'll have me. I want us to fix this place up. I remember the night we ended up here. You've already got great ideas for it—like the trim color."

Aaron opened his mouth, as if he were searching for the right words but couldn't quite find them.

Caleb pressed on. There was certainly no stopping now. "Come on inside. I'd love to hear more about what you want to do to our home." He pulled the keys from his pocket and unlocked the front door. He gestured for Aaron to go first and heard his breath catch as he crossed the threshold. The interior was brightly lit given the sunny day.

"I feel like I'm in a movie," Aaron finally said. "This can't be real. Maybe I was hit on the head by a ball during recess or something." He slowly spun around, taking in the empty room.

As Caleb had hoped, Aaron's focus was immediately

drawn to the mantel. Caleb joined him, standing by his side at the fireplace.

"You're just full of surprises." Aaron said, picking up the framed photo. Tears fell as Aaron looked at the image of the kiss that had been captured in the park. He carefully set the frame down, jerked Caleb to him, and kissed him hard. Caleb met the kiss head-on, loving its aggressive hunger and how the friction of their beards felt.

"I love you, Caleb," Aaron said when he broke away. "I do. I should've said it back the other night."

They cried, kissed, and held each other tightly.

"I love you so much," Aaron said between smooches. "I'm sorry I was so stupid. I should've just followed my heart. I'm never going to let you go."

"Good. Because I don't want to be let go. And you weren't stupid. You were hurt. This starts something new, for both of us. And if you ever feel like something's not right between us, tell me. I promise I'll do the same with you."

"Promise," Aaron said, wiping at his damp cheeks as his tears finally began to subside. "You know what else this room needs? That painting of the lake we looked at. There's no view of the lake from here, but that picture would be—"

"Perfect," they said together.

"Right over the fireplace," Aaron said.

Caleb nodded. "Come with me." He led them to the kitchen, where two plastic glasses sat on the counter. From the fridge, he pulled a bottle of champagne.

"You really thought of everything." Aaron couldn't stop smiling.

"Full disclosure," Caleb said as he worked on the cork. "The champagne was Grant's idea. But the rest of it? All mine and all for you."

The cork released with a pop, spraying its contents

across the kitchen. Caleb poured two glasses, and they each took one.

"Thank you for taking the leap. I'll do everything I can so you don't regret it."

"Thank God you were persistent. I can't believe what you've done today. I look forward to all that comes next."

They clicked the plastic together and drank.

"How did you pull all this off?" Aaron asked, refilling their glasses.

"I won't sugarcoat it—money and an assistant can get a lot of things done fast. I'm glad you like it. I'm pretty sure I'll never be able to top it."

"I can't imagine how you could. This is beyond anything I could've dreamed of."

"You make me so happy." Caleb leaned in and stole a champagne-flavored kiss from the man he adored. He then pulled back so he could look Aaron in the eye. He took a deep breath. "So this is home base, effective immediately. New York is work. You and Foster Gove are home. We can spend the summer settling and figuring out how we want to manage things when next season starts."

"I want you to know that I heard everything you said in your apartment, even if I was stupidly fighting against it. I admit I might have looked into some of those relationships you mentioned. There's this guy who coaches in Pittsburgh but lives in Dallas, and he has a wife and kids. If he can make that craziness work, you and I can surely find a way."

Caleb laughed. "We're going to be fine. I bet we'll end up seeing so much of each other that you'll be like 'please, give me a break.'"

"I can't see that happening," Aaron said, then took a sip from his glass.

"Just so you know, I fully intend to ask you to marry me."

Aaron coughed and sputtered the champagne he hadn't quite finished swallowing. Caleb gently patted Aaron on the back until the coughing fit subsided.

"I didn't mean to get you that choked up."

"It's okay," Aaron insisted, setting the plastic champagne flute aside.

"I'm not proposing, at least not yet, anyway. Asking you right now, in this moment, wouldn't be fair." He took Aaron's hands in his own. "This is a lot to take in—the house, our new lives together—and I get that, so I'm not going to pressure you. But I want you to know that when it comes to us, I am one hundred percent all in."

Caleb waited for a response, but Aaron remained quiet. He could usually read the emotion in Aaron's expressive eyes, but at the moment, his expression was frustratingly neutral. Had Caleb misread the situation? Was it all too much? Had his grand gesture backfired?

"What if I asked you?" Aaron said.

Caleb wasn't sure he understood. "Asked me what?"

Aaron gave an exasperated huff. "To marry me."

"Wait a second. Really?"

Aaron nodded. "These past few days, I've had a chance to think about what I want out of life. I realized I was letting things in my past control my future. I was afraid of getting hurt again, afraid to take a chance and truly move forward. I don't want fear to ever hold me back again. What I want, *all* I want, is you, Caleb."

"It means so much to hear you say that."

"I'm one hundred percent all in too. Will you marry me?"

"God, yes. Of course I will."

Caleb grabbed hold of Aaron, wrapped him in an embrace, and twirled him around. He let out whoop of joy, the sound echoing against the bare walls of their new house. A home they'd they make theirs and fill with love. Caleb set him down and took Aaron's handsome face in his hands, kissing him thoroughly.

They were interrupted by the buzz of Aaron's phone vibrating. Caleb's phone also chirped to life. They ignored them until both phones went off again.

Aaron pulled back, chuckling. "One guess who that is."

"I don't think I have to." Caleb took his phone from his pocket and showed Aaron the screen. "She never was patient." They looked at the screen together.

One of you better tell me something soon. The anticipation is killing me.

"Are we keeping this a secret or do we tell her?" Aaron asked.

"I have no intention of keeping this news under wraps. Do you want to text her or should I?"

"You can do it."

Caleb typed: *You'll have a brother-in-law soon.* "Look good?" He showed it to Aaron.

"Perfect."

Caleb clicked Send, put the phone on the counter, and pulled Aaron close so they could get back to the kissing.

They ignored her replies.

EPILOGUE

"Babe," Caleb shouted from the living room, "hurry up. The commercial is almost over."

"I'm almost done," Aaron called out as he pulled the bag of popcorn from the microwave and emptied the contents into a large bowl.

They'd been working on the house together since they returned from Caleb's championship win. In the lead-up to the championships, Aaron had overseen some of the remodeling of the house—refinishing the floors, fresh paint where it was needed, better kitchen appliances. The painting of the pond that Caleb loved so much hung over the fireplace in the living room. Meanwhile, the scandalous paparazzi picture of their park kiss and the "World's Best Tutor" trophy had a home on the mantel.

Aaron turned off the kitchen light and joined Caleb on the couch that had just been delivered that afternoon. Aaron snuggled in close to him, balancing the bowl of popcorn between them, as they prepared to watch Dimitri's interview. The online live stream of NY1 was the only way to see it in Foster Grove.

As Aaron reached for a handful of popcorn, Caleb leaned even closer. "I like how that engagement ring looks on your finger."

Aaron glanced at his hand and admired the platinum band that now adorned his ring finger. "As it turns out, not only is my fiancé an excellent hockey player, he has superlative taste in men's jewelry."

"Aren't you a lucky fellow," Caleb teased, nibbling Aaron's earlobe.

"Okay, Romeo, let's put that idea on hold until after the show," he said, focusing their attention back to the television.

"Welcome back to *Sports on One*. Joining us is Dimitri Stanislov, one of the stars of the newly crowned Stanley Cup championship team," the interviewer said, introducing Dimitri. "Congratulations. You helped bring the Cup back to New York for the first time since 1994."

Dimitri's smile was wolfish, cocky. "It was an incredible experience lifting the Cup in front of the amazing home crowd after game seven last week, and to share it again with all the fans at the parade just a few days ago."

Caleb had secured Aaron and Pam VIP seats for the parade. In the grandstands at City Hall, they had screamed so loudly for Caleb when he stood at the podium, they were hoarse for several days after. It was during that same trip that Caleb signed a new five-year deal with the Rangers because the team wanted to lock in their Stanley Cup winning captain.

"He loves this stuff," Caleb said. Dimitri's confidence in front of the camera couldn't be denied. "I'd give him all the media interviews, if I could. He really eats it up."

"It was an interesting run to the finals," the interviewer continued as a series of highlights played on the in-studio monitor. "Sweeping Boston in the first round, only to take six games to knock out Pittsburgh for the conference championship. Then it was seven to finally defeat San Jose, and that included three overtime games."

"San Jose did not want to go down quietly, that's for sure." Dimitri laughed. "Those were intense games, especially on the road. Our team stepped up just a little bit more, and it made the difference. It was thrilling how it turned out."

"Let's shift for a moment and talk about your captain and best friend." An image of Caleb and Aaron that had been taken on the ice at The Garden after the Rangers win appeared on screen. Caleb was lifting the cup over their heads while Aaron had his arm around him. They were both smiling from ear to ear.

"Oh, geez, that picture just keeps coming back," Caleb said, momentarily covering his eyes.

"You look adorable." Aaron leaned over and kissed Caleb's cheek.

"I'm glad you think so. You'd think the team photographer would make sure I didn't look like a complete goofball. Look at that ridiculous smile."

"Like I said. Adorable."

Caleb looked to Aaron and playfully stuck his tongue out, which Aaron responded to by leaning over and kissing it.

They turned their attention back to the screen as Dimitri spoke. "I couldn't be more thrilled for Caleb. It's hard not to be when you see how tremendously happy he is. You saw how he was smiling in that photo." The image reappeared, and Caleb groaned. "That's it. Look at that smile. He's got the Cup and he's got a wonderful man. My friend deserves all of it."

"I'm going to kill him," Caleb said through a sigh.

"Aww," Aaron said, snuggling against Caleb while making sure the popcorn didn't fall. "But he said you've got a wonderful man."

"That's true." Caleb repositioned himself so he could wrap his arm around Aaron. "I do."

"And what are your plans now that the season's over?" the interviewer asked.

"I'm taking the Cup home to Denver for an event at my high school, and I'll spend some time there with my family. The most important thing on the calendar, though, is Caleb's August wedding. I'm honored that he asked me to stand with him. I'm sure it's going to be epic. Come fall, Caleb and I will also do some speaking gigs to support the You Can Play initiative at a few high schools in the Northeast."

"We certainly send Caleb best wishes on his wedding. And we're already looking forward to what you, Caleb, and the rest of the team bring to The Garden next year. Thanks for being with us, Dimitri. We'll be right back with more *Sports on One* right after this."

As the commercial started, Aaron reached for the remote and clicked a button to start Netflix. "So, what's it going to be?" he asked as he clicked through the menu of programs.

"I'm thinking," Caleb said as he moved the popcorn to the coffee table, "maybe it's not a Netflix night after all." He took the remote from Aaron and placed it next to the bowl. "It might be better if it's just us." With a very fluid movement, Caleb straddled Aaron and leaned in for a kiss.

"Works for me," Aaron said, his words muffled between kisses.

THANKS FOR READING *The Hockey Player's Heart!* Reviews are an incredibly valuable to spreading the word about great books. Please consider leaving a review about *The Hockey Player's Heart* on your favorite retailer or review site.

ALSO BY JEFF ADAMS

Hockey Romance

Head in the Game

The Hockey Player's Heart (co-written with Will Knauss)

The Hockey Player's Snow Day

Keeping Kyle (A Hockey Allies Bachelor Bid Romance)

Rivals

On Stage Series

Dancing for Him

Love's Opening Night

More Romance Titles

A Sound Beginning

Room Service

Somewhere on Mackinac

Summer Heat

Young Adult Titles

Each of these are available in ebook, paperback and audiobook

Codename: Winger series

Tracker Hacker (includes the bonus short story _A Very Winger Christmas_)

Schooled

Audio Assault

Netminder

Other Young Adult Titles

Flipping for Him

ABOUT JEFF ADAMS

Jeff Adams has written stories since he was in middle school and became a published author in 2009 when his first short stories were published. He writes both gay romance and LGBTQ young adult fiction...and there's usually a hockey player at the center of the story.

Jeff lives in central California with his husband of more than twenty years, Will. Some of his favorite things include the musicals *Rent* and *[title of show]*, the Detroit Red Wings and Pittsburgh Penguins hockey teams, and the reality TV competition *So You Think You Can Dance*. He, of course, loves to read, but there isn't enough space to list out his favorite books.

Jeff and Will are also podcasters. The *Big Gay Fiction Podcast* is a weekly show devoted to gay romance as well as pop culture. New episodes come out every Monday at BigGayFictionPodcast.com.

Learn more about Jeff, his books and find his social media links at JeffAdamsWrites.com. From the website you can also sign up for his newsletter to get a free ebook of *The Hockey Player's Snow Day*, as well serialized stories, previews of new books, book recommendations and more!

ABOUT WILL KNAUSS

Will Knauss is a child of the seventies. When he wasn't twirling around on the playground (like Lynda Carter from *Wonder Woman*), he wrote stories and performed plays for family members. Enthusiasm for his theatrical presentations varied. Before becoming an author, Will's work experience ranged from hotel housekeeper to retail clerk. While living in New York, he even worked as a Wax Museum tour guide.

In 1995 he asked the man who would eventually become his husband on a date. No Netflix and chill for them, though, remember, this was the Dark Ages (aka the midnineties). They went to an actual theater to see the John Carpenter remake of *Village of the Damned*. They have been inseparable ever since.

Each week, Will shares his love of gay romance fiction with the listeners of the *Big Gay Fiction Podcast*, a show he co-created with his husband and fellow author, Jeff Adams.

You can keep up with Will at WillKnauss.com and check out the podcast at BigGayFictionPodcast.com.

Lightning Source UK Ltd.
Milton Keynes UK
UKHW020637260821
389510UK00009B/290